W9-CSY-572

New World: Rising

Jennifer Wilson

For my parents,
whose love and support
taught me to believe in myself and to
never give up on my dreams.

Text copyright © 2014 Jennifer Wilson
All rights reserved.
First Edition: August 2014

The characters and events portrayed in this book are
fictitious. Any similarity to real persons, living or dead, is
coincidental and not intended by the author.

Wilson, Jennifer 1984-
New World: Rising: a novel / by Jennifer Wilson.-1st ed.

Summary: When seventeen-year-old orphan rogue Phoenix
saves a child from a Tribal hunting party, her life is turned
upside down when the Subversive subsequently capture her.
However, despite their lack of compassion they may just hold
the key to her forgotten past.

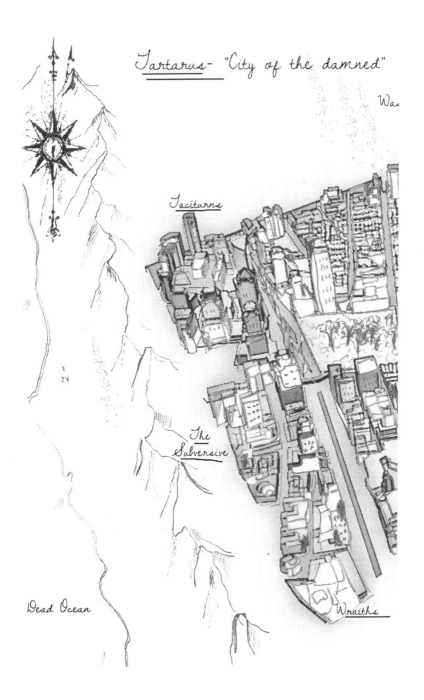

Tartarus- "City of the damned"

Wa...

Taciturns

The
Subversive

Dead Ocean

Wraiths

CONTENTS

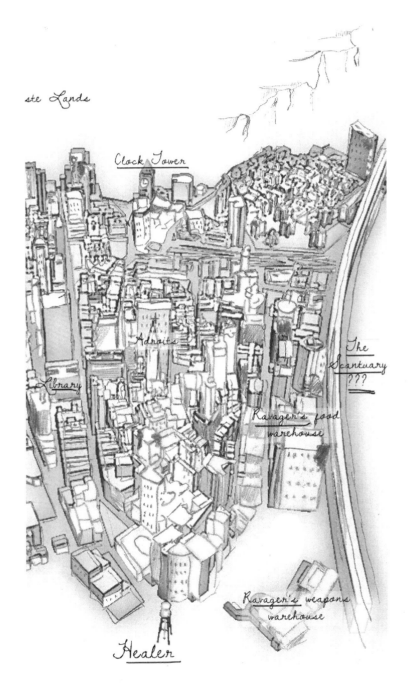

ste Lands

Clock Tower

Adroits

Library

The
Scantuary
???

Ravager's food
warehouse

Ravager's weapons
warehouse

Healer

Adroits

Smart clever group, set traps that result in high payout with low physical involvement

Colors: Purple & gold

Markings: Bald heads (both male and female)

Taciturns

Silent, deceptive- have planted their spies in other Tribes

Colors: maroon, grey

Markings: tattoos- under cover Tribesman have only the bottom of their tongue tattooed

Scavengers

Thief's / rats of the city.
They scurry behind other
Tribes reaping the profits
of their kills.
When spoils
run slim they
pick off the weak,
turning on each other
just as often as they would a
stranger. Their motto is "Sleep
with one eye open."

Colors: brown,
filthy

Markings: missing
teeth, poor hygiene, dirty

Stole from my parents.

Wraiths

The ghosts of the city, rarely seen - collect victim's left hands

<u>Colors</u>: white, blue

<u>Markings</u>: Wear hand bones arround their necks, animal pelts, & war paint. Look wild.

Ravagers

The most loud and violent tribe. Hunt people for sport. Easiest source ~~of~~ for food and weapons.

<u>Killed my parents.</u>

<u>Colors</u>: black, red

<u>Markings</u>: tons of piercings & wears mostly leather

1. HAUNTED

The wind slapped my face as I looked down on the city below me. The scarce figures moving in the streets looked like ants. Their small bodies skittered through the shadows, avoiding the few street lamps that still worked. The dark meant protection, safety. Those amber pools of light meant exposing yourself, being seen, and no one wanted to be seen out in the open. Not unless they had a death wish.

Death sounded nice sometimes. It would be so... easy.

I leaned out farther from the ledge, rising on my toes to support the shifting weight. One little movement, one second of letting go and it could all be over. I wouldn't even have to watch my impending collision. I could just close my eyes and wait for the pavement to claim me. I doubted I would even feel it. My consciousness would surely be gone before even the Scavengers found me.

I could jump.

I wouldn't be the first to give up, to want out.

A cold gust of wind pushed the hood back from my face. I leaned backwards, letting my heels fall to meet the solid cement again. It would be easy, *too* easy. My mother's last words echoed in my mind. *"Be strong, survive."*

1

It had been six years since I watched my parents' murders. Six years of hiding, of surviving this god-forsaken place. Six years could make people forget, lose themselves, but it only sharpened my hate, chiseling their deaths, their last words into every fiber of my being.

"Be strong, survive."

Those three words made me get up, made me eat, and made me keep moving. And those same three words haunted me everyday.

I closed my eyes, seeing my mother's face. She was beautiful. I always looked too much like her, but her face was soft. That softness was lost on me. I was hardened. I could still feel the iron bars of the grate pressed against my palms, see my father's scared face as he lowered me into the storm drain, hear my mother's voice as she slipped the backpack over my shoulders. I watched silently from the prison where my parents placed me as the Ravagers took their lives, my knuckles bleeding as I pressed them to my mouth to keep from screaming. I saw my father bleed out as he watched them rape his wife. I listened to my mother fight back before they took her life too. I fought to free myself, to save her, but the grate was too heavy and I was too weak. Later, I watched as the Scavengers came for them, stealing the clothing off my parents' backs while their bodies were still warm.

I thought I would die in that storm drain, trapped forever, but one of the Scavengers saw me— and for reasons I still do not understand— he pulled up the grate and dragged me out. I should have screamed or fought him, but I remembered my mother's words and instead just held his gaze. He seemed fascinated by my boldness before turning his back to me. I watched as he pulled my father's shoes over his own stained and tattered socks.

"Life's harsh out here kid, it's every man for himself. But don't say nobody never did nothing for you." Without a second glance at me, he tossed my father's pocketknife at my feet and left me standing alone in a dark alley.

2

I was eleven.

After that day I was on my own. I never trusted anyone, never sought friends. My father had left his journal in the backpack. It contained plans, ideas for surviving in the city we called Tartarus— or as the Ancient Greeks referred to it: "The dungeon of the damned."

I scoured his notes, following them devoutly. And I survived.

I stepped down from the ledge of the building. I was a survivor, not a coward. Death would not be so easy for me. As many times as I had thought about giving up, stepping off a building or walking out into the daylight unarmed, I could never commit. As much as I wanted death, I couldn't surrender to it. For my parents' sake, more than mine, I had to try. I had to keep going. I owed that much to them.

I checked my father's pocket watch. It was one of the other few things he had left in the backpack. It was a handsome, old hand-wound timepiece. It wasn't much, but I loved the old watch. No batteries meant no failure and power was a scarce thing in Tartarus. I watched the frail hands tick. The sun would be coming up soon which meant the Tribes would take control of the streets once again.

The Tribes ruled Tartarus. While they prowled mostly during they daytime, their power was unequivocal.

Join or die— that was the way of the city.

There were five Tribes to choose from. The five lesser evils as I liked to think of them. Each had their own defining virtues— if you could call them that— but they were all murderers, all tyrants seeking power.

The Adroits were probably the lesser of all the evils. They were the cleverest of the Tribes, keeping their hands clean by their own standards. They sought death and power, but rarely got close to the dirty work. Adroits set numerous traps throughout Tartarus— bombs that could take out a city block, IEDs that would take a man out at the knees leaving him to bleed out, pits that could swallow a person into the sea of waiting spikes at the bottom. Yes, they rarely killed a person with their own bare hands, but their death toll was still high.

Equally as cunning and incredibly more deceitful were the Taciturns, but unlike the Adroits they were not afraid to get their hands dirty. They moved like silent shadows. Rarely heard, but their presence was everywhere. Tribe wars rarely started or ended without the Taciturns' involvement. How they managed to get into the minds of other Tribes perplexed me, but somehow they always seemed to know everything.

The Wraiths were even more of a mystery; rarely seen, they were called the ghosts of the city. Few knew where they gathered or what their true numbers were, but their reputation preceded them. No one survived an attack to tell about it, but the aftermaths were enough to strike fear in even the darkest heart. Each murder was marked by the removal of the victim's left hand. As the victim's blood spilled out, the murderer marked his or her kill with a handprint pressed into their victim's freshly pooling blood. Wraiths always claimed their killings, marking each massacre with pride.

The Scavengers were the least threatening, but they were the scum of the city. The vile rats that slithered amongst sewage. They scurried behind other Tribes, reaping the profits of their kills. When spoils ran slim they would pick off the weak, turning on each other just as often as they would a stranger. Their motto was "Sleep with one eye open." They were also the number one contributor to the city's lost orphans. The Scavengers reproduced like the rodents they were, but didn't possess a nurturing bone in their disease-ridden bodies. Any child born in their tribe was usually left for dead. If the child could walk on its own, it could fend for itself. I never forgave them for robbing my parents, even if I was spared. My hatred for those filthy rats was only overpowered by my hate for one other Tribe. The Ravagers.

Scavengers might have taken my parents' last belongings, but it was the Ravagers who took their lives. They were the largest and most deadly Tribe. Aside from their

4

overwhelming numbers, they ran purely on their ids. Always seeking out instant gratification for their basic urges, needs, and desires. If they wanted something, they took it. The Ravagers feared no one, took what they wanted and lived like death could never find them. They raped women, killed children and generally took pleasure in others' pain. Humanity was becoming a dying breed under their reign.

Join or die.

Those were the rules of *their* city, not mine. I may live here now, but it was not where I was born.

I wouldn't play by their rules.

I wouldn't sell my soul to the devil, even if it meant living longer. And if you won't play with the devil you had better learn to hide from him.

The way I saw it, I had two choices. Go underground or take to the sky. In the end I figured it was better to see from above rather than to bury myself. In truth, there really wasn't much of a choice. The smell of the underground reminded me of the storm drain, of my parents' deaths, the hot air swirling around my feet as the faint hint of sewage and decay clung to my nostrils. I gagged just thinking about it.

As an outcast, I never stayed more than one consecutive day in any of my refuges. As morning threatened I would pack up my things and roll my twenty-sided dice. It was a strange dice, red with white faded letters on each side. But to me, each letter meant a different safe house, a different place to hide. The real security was in randomness. Without patterns a person is harder to track and the dice proved to be my greatest ally in remaining unpredictable.

I watched the red dice bounce to a halt falling on the letter B. I smiled. Tonight's safe house was my favorite and it had been nearly a month since I had been there. Snatching up the dice, I slung my bag over my shoulder and took off at a run.

As always, I kept to the rooftops. I ran lightly, careful not to fall, careful not to give my location away. Here, in the remnants of what was once a great city, the decrepit buildings lay close together. While their frames held true, most of their insides had been gutted. Torn apart over the years by Tribe wars, animals and time. Unless you could scale a drainpipe, brave an abandoned elevator shaft or climb the eroded brick on the side of a building, most rooftops were unreachable. It didn't help that I had been slowly deconstructing most avenues to get skyward over the years. There were now few buildings that allowed access upwards and I knew them all.

I leapt over the small gap between buildings just as the first drop fell. I glared at the sky before pulling up my hood and picking up speed.

"Rain…" I grumbled to myself.

This wasn't the drinking kind, the kind that replenished the earth. What was once the world's lifeline, now reeked of toxicity. If drank, it would surely kill a person and if caught in it for too long, your skin would pay the price. I only had to get the blistering rash once to know that rain was to be avoided.

I came to the padlocked door just as the sky opened up. Quickly, I pulled the pins in the door's hinge. Locks kept most people out but only because they never thought to remove the hinges. I dragged the heavy door closed behind me, feeling a weight slide off my shoulders as it shut.

Pushing the rain-soaked hood back from my face, I started forward in the dark. My feet knew the way even when my eyes couldn't see it. I let my fingers trace the wall, until they found open air. Dodging sideways, I ducked into the hole just big enough for my body. The air duct had gotten tighter over the years as I had grown but my progress was still uninhibited. After twenty feet or so, I felt the grated vent against my palms. I pressed my ear to the perforated surface and listened for a sixty count. Upon hearing nothing, I pushed. Carefully, I lowered myself through the opening until my feet found a solid surface. My chest felt tight in the darkness, but I knew precautions must be taken before I could light a torch. When sloppiness can cost you your life, you learn not to be sloppy.

6

I pressed the vent closed, my fingers tracing the cardboard outline covering it. Taking great care, I stepped down from my perch and took seven calculated steps forward. As before with the vent, I traced the door, ensuring all the gaps were still covered. Once I was confident no light would escape, I pulled the torch from my bag.

I had to crank the handle fifteen times, and then clicked the switch. The light was an odd shade of green, but it was still a light. Choices of light sources were slim here and although this bulb cast everything in a sickly hue, the benefit was that it would probably outlive me. Despite my distaste for the green glow, it was still a welcome friend in the darkness. The light was oddly fitting here, the wan illumination the perfect representation of the city of Tartarus. Vile and repulsive and yet, somehow, it had become home.

The room was exactly as I had left it. At one point it must have been a supply closet or something of the sort, but it was void of any cleaning supplies or unnecessary boxes. The old shelving I had used as a ladder was now covered in books with a few surplus food boxes mixed in. I tried to keep a small stash in every hostel for days like this when the rain trapped me inside. I threw my bag down, hung up my coat to dry in the corner and ran my hands over the books' bindings. Pulling a familiar leather-bound book from the shelf, I held it to my nose.

I loved that smell. In all of my adventures, nothing ever smelled quite like an old book. This one was by a Charles Dickens, entitled *A Tale of Two Cities*. It was one of my favorites, not just because of its characters and story, but because I remembered my parents reading it to me as a child. One of the few memories I had. Touching the book, reading over its words made me feel like they were still with me, like I wasn't alone. That's why I loved this refuge more than any other, not for its location in the city or its safety, but for what was contained within its walls. Outside this storage closest was what remained of the Old World's library. During my visits

7

here, I would brave the open aisles and steal books. The main floor of the library was desolate. Few people knew how to read anymore and most books had been stolen for kindling during the winters. Fortunately though, the Adroits had blown up the stairs leading to the upper levels at some point so most of the books there remained intact. I had collected many of my favorites, but my reading choices were becoming limited. Maybe after some sleep, I would venture out for new material.

I placed the book back with its brothers and took inventory of my supplies.

There were two bottles of fresh water, three empty bottles, five water purifying tablets, two packs of dried fruit, two military grade MREs and a rare can of pears. It had expired a year ago, but a girl could not afford to be picky. I wrote down everything in my notebook, logging what I would need to restock. My supplies were running low.

Grabbing a bottle of water, a MRE and the can of pears, I settled into the makeshift cot I had stuffed in the corner. The MREs were never bad, but they weren't great either. The hardest part was usually finding a way to heat them. If I placed the bag over my torch lantern, I could usually get a lukewarm meal in about thirty minutes, give or take. I poured in a measured amount of water and balanced the bag precariously on top of the glowing light.

While my meal warmed, I took my father's notebook out. Idly, I ran my fingertips over the four-inch scar behind my right ear as I looked over the pages. His handwriting was so small and precise to a fault. My scrawl looked childlike next to his. The notebook was filled with his words. A good portion of it was written in a code he had taught me. While I could remember how to read the script, I couldn't remember what he had called it. Latin or Larin or something like that. My mind could never latch onto its name, but as long as I knew how to read it, I didn't really care. Lists spanned the pages, ideas that had filtered through his mind. Places to seek shelter, places to avoid, people who might trade, things to remember, old ways

8

that should never be forgotten. Things like the written word, where we came from, what had happened to the world before our time.

In the Old World, before The Devastation, planet earth was escalating. Science had changed the world— in some ways for the better, in other ways toward its detriment. Science saved lives that would have been otherwise damned, constantly cheating death. The world's population was soaring. But Mother Nature got her revenge. When The Devastation came she got her comeuppance. For every life science had saved, she reaped thousands.

There were many names for what happened to the world. Some called it the Armageddon or the apocalypse; others saw it as nature's way of purging itself. Either way, the destruction of the world was devastating. It started with the earthquakes. While cities fell into rubble, other parts of the earth opened up. Once dormant volcanoes awoke, searing the sky and smothering the land. Then the water came. The earth took back its land, drowning most of the world. Oceans swallowed continents whole, countries that once shared borders became islands and islands disappeared never to be seen again.

Governments fell apart and panic ruled. So many lives were lost, technologies destroyed. Life as the human race knew it ceased to exist. But, as with all great travesties, there came hope. Survivors banded together, The Wall was built and The Sanctuary was created. Those who sought security and equality were welcomed to The Sanctuary with open arms. Those who sought power and dominance were left to Tartarus. Cultures ceased to exist and races blended together but the human race still found a way to divide itself. The Sanctuary formed a civilization that ostracized the world outside its walls, and that abandoned world formed the Tribes to survive. This was the New World.

I traced my father's script, wishing for the one answer he didn't leave me. Why did he make our family leave The

Sanctuary?

No matter how many times I reread his pages or how many times I traced his words, the answer was never there. I wished I could remember something, anything from before the night of my parents' deaths. But it was as if all those memories had died with them. I think maybe it was my mind's way of protecting itself. I would get flashes of them reading me books or looking up at my mother as I held her hand. But that's all they were. Flashes. I set his journal aside and opened the can of pears, relishing the sweet smell. I pulled one out, toasting myself before taking a bite.

"Happy Birthday."

2. SURVIVING

I awoke with a start, my arms flailing outward, as the scream caught in my throat. It only took seconds to recognize my surroundings, to calm my racing heart. This was how I awoke every morning, every morning since my parents died. After years I managed to restrain the scream, awakening before it escaped my lips. Screaming in the night could get you found, screaming during the daytime would get you killed.

I checked my father's watch in the green light. It was nearly three in the afternoon. There were still hours until dark. I knew I would have to stock up more food before I left for my next refuge, but scavenging during the daytime wasn't an option.

Thumbing through my book collections, I felt uninspired and bored, having already read them so many times. I thought about trying to sleep longer but my mind was too awake. After eating a breakfast of dried apples, I made a plan to grow my personal library. Aside from needing something else to distract my mind, books always proved a good source of trade. Those few of us who defied the Tribes kept to ourselves and stayed quiet. We never gathered, nor really ever trusted one another. But when goods ran scarce, trades were not uncommon. It was finding the *right* recluses to trade with that was key. One wrong choice and you could easily find yourself with empty hands and a knife in your back. A select few of my merchants knew how to read and those that didn't, never turned down good kindling.

Rifling through my few belongings, I decided to leave my larger backpack behind. It was too heavy and often cumbersome while crawling through the vents. I would only need a small tote big enough to carry books. My revolver lay on the mattress in its holster. I eyed it, speculating if it was needed. I always took it with me outside or to hunt for food, but no one ever came in the library anymore. I had seen a few rats and the occasional wild dogs on the floors below, but none of them ever bothered me. Instead I slid my knife into my hip sheath and climbed up the shelves to the vent.

As always, I moved with great caution, careful to never make a sound and always listening for others. But like usual, the building was empty. After nearly ten minutes of crawling, I saw light shining up through the galvanized steel. Cautiously I pressed my ear to the vent while holding my breath.

Nothing.

I smiled and pushed open the grate before sliding out onto the top of a bookshelf. Before descending I scanned the rows, my keen eyes looking for any trace of movement, foreign color or moved shelving. Nothing had changed since I was here last. Several of the books I had discarded still lay on the floor where I had dumped them, uninterested.

Relaxing a bit, I took a deep breath. The room was massive, filled with rows upon rows of abandoned books. It smelled like aged paper, and earth from the destroyed floors below. I loved that smell. Soundlessly, I climbed down the metal shelf I had perched on and headed for my favorite sections.

First I stopped by the romance section— business first, then pleasure. These were my least favorite kind of book. People fell into whirlwind romance, swept up with sex and passion. I didn't believe in love, it was a wasted emotion that could get you killed. People did foolish things in the name of love. While I detested these books, they were generally thick and most of my allies didn't care about the content as long as they burned.

I never made friends, not even with my allies. There were those I could barter with safely, and those I couldn't, I stole from. I never stole from the dead. Rationally it made more sense to take from the dead; after all it wasn't like they would be using anything any more. But the thought made me nauseous, reminding me too much of watching my parents' murders. Instead I traded with a few recluses and targeted the Tribes' storage facilities for the rest. I never felt guilty stealing from them.

Blindly grabbing a few thick books, I tossed them into my bag and moved on to the educational section. I browsed the titles looking for books on survival and warfare. After skimming their backs I took two of the most promising titles before moving on to the fiction section. I loved this section the most. The books here provided an escape, a place to let my mind wander free and find friends. Not real friends, but friends I could care about without having to commit to. Once I had opened a book and read its pages, those characters could never be taken away from me. Even if the books were burned, they would still live on in my mind. They couldn't die or betray you, friends on paper proved much more lucrative than real ones.

This section was also the largest, and after years of perusing its shelves I had only just scratched the surface. Leisurely, I moved through the rows looking for authors I recognized or titles that called to me. Upon finding one of interest I would pull it from the shelf and read the back cover or the first few pages. Anything of interest was added to my collection. Everything else got added to the growing pile on the floor. I was so immersed in the pages of a potential gem that I almost didn't hear them.

Two voices were making their way toward me, speaking

in hushed tones.

"Shut up. I swear I heard something up here."

"If I scaled that damn rope for nothing, I swear I will slit your throat myself."

Every muscle in my body tensed as the distinctly male voices drifted through the aisles. Careful not to make a sound, I slipped the book into my bag and peeked through a gap in the books. Their backs were turned to me, the black leather of their coats splattered in red. Both men were hulking in size, my head probably even with their chests. The taller one had a red mohawk with feathers dangling from it. The other was bald with deep scars that covered the entire left side of his head like angry red fissures. Both of them had an obscene amount of metal piercings protruding from their skin. My hair rose on end.

Ravagers.

What the hell were they doing here? Panic prickled in the pit of my stomach. The vent leading to safety was nearly five rows over across the aisle; there was no way to make it there without being seen. Why hadn't I brought my gun? I cursed myself as their eyes scanned the empty rows.

"I smell *fear*." One of them taunted, his gruff voice no longer whispering.

They cackled with delight.

I swallowed hard. Even if it was just a farce to scare me, it was working, my pulse accelerating. Punching the other in the shoulder, the one with the mohawk motioned for them to spilt off. My ears began to ring as they moved to either side of my row and progressed towards me. I was trapped. My eyes instantly searched for another route of escape or a place to hide. As their footsteps moved closer, I began to silently climb.

"Here kitty, kitty. Come on out, we won't hurt you." The higher voice crooned.

"Much." The deep voice replied before they broke into another round of laughter.

Perched on the center of the shelf I waited until they

were about even with my aisle. As they turned the corner, I swung my body over the top pressing myself flat against the metal surface. All they had to do was look up and I would be dead. I cursed myself again for leaving my gun. How could I have been so foolish?

I pressed my face to the dusty metal surface, preparing to run at a moment's notice. My hand closed over the hilt of my knife. If I could injure one, I might have a chance of outrunning the other. I stared at the vent several aisles over. I could jump the gaps easily and stick to the shelf tops, but only if they didn't—I heard the familiar click and my heart sank as I finished the thought. They had a gun. A hulking brute I could outrun, but a bullet? The chances were thin.

"They're here somewhere. I feel it." The mohawk whispered again.

My heart pounded in my ears as I prepared to launch myself into motion. Aim for the eye, aim for the eye I reminded myself. As my wrist twitched to free my knife, a crash erupted from the other side of the library.

The shelf I lay on shook, nearly knocking me off as one of the Ravagers clipped the corner in their pursuit of the noise. Rowdily, they blundered down the aisles whooping and hollering their battle cry. Without hesitation I sprang to my feet and sprinted across the bookshelves as they disappeared. My feet slid on the dusty surfaces, but managed to keep their purchase. Another crash emitted from the floor below. I turned, launching across the main aisle toward the vent. My foot slipped on the edge, my shin colliding with the sharp edge as I caught myself. An involuntary cry escaped as pain exploded through my leg.

"Get off the rope you idiot! They're still up here!" A voice screamed, coming closer again.

Limping, I dragged myself the last few steps. Smashing my fist into the vent I knocked it open and pulled myself inside. As I yanked the grate closed I drew my face back from the light, watching as the two Ravagers came back into view.

They were both sweating and obviously enraged.

"NO ONE IS HERE DAMN IT!"

I clenched my jaw as mohawk turned his gun on scar face and pulled the trigger. The bullet pierced his arm, blood spraying on the books behind him as he screamed. I couldn't watch the fight that ensued, the sounds of their fists like slapping meat echoing in the vent. While I didn't want to watch I also knew moving wasn't an option. One sound and they would surely fire a round in the ceiling just for fun. Closing my eyes I pressed my face to the cool metal and covered my ears. The sound of colliding flesh wasn't entirely drowned out, but it was at least dulled. The minutes pressed on like hours until they eventually worked off their anger and stumbled away. Even after their voices had faded I lay still. After nearly twenty minutes of silence I finally crawled my way back to the storage closet.

My leg throbbed when I hopped down from the shelving. There was something warm pooling in the top of my shoe. Carefully sitting, I turned my lantern on and pulled up my pant leg. A six-inch gash ran down my shin, specks of raw white flesh were visible under the flowing blood. I took a deep breath and let my head fall against the wall.

I had been so stupid, *so* careless. I was getting too comfortable and it nearly cost me my life. Grabbing a bottle of water I splashed it on a rag and pressed it to the raw skin. Air hissed out my teeth as my body shook with pain, but I forced myself to keep breathing.

I would remember this.

I would remember what my carelessness had cost me. What it could have cost me if something hadn't fallen when it did. I was sure it was a part of the building caving in or rotted ceiling tiles crashing to the floor. I had gotten lucky, but one should never be so stupid to rely solely on luck.

My body stopped shaking as the pain lessened, the endorphins now flowing through my system. My pain, the scar I would surely bear would be a vivid reminder to stay vigilant.

Carefully, I wrapped my leg to staunch the bleeding. The cut was not deep, but skin over shallow bone seemed to bleed a lot. I dug in my bag and came up empty. My medical salves were gone and infection was a great risk. I would have to see The Healer.

I never learned her real name, but most of us went by false ones anyway. She was an ancient woman with thinning grey hair and a withered face with creased lines deep as craters. Her gnarled hands were frightening when they touched you, but her medicines were good. I would have to find food and herbs to trade with her. And unfortunately, there was only one place I could procure both those things. The Ravagers' supply container. It was a heavily guarded warehouse on the edge of The Wall. I had planned to go there tonight anyway, but an injured leg was sure to slow me down.

I couldn't stay here another night, but if I rolled the dice there was no guarantee I would land on a nearby safe house. If I wanted to be hidden before dark I would have to pick one close to The Healer, even if it broke all of my rules. Mentally I went through my list searching for an easily accessible safe house. The school. It was some kind of an educational housing in the Old World. It was filled with abandoned rooms and decrepit hallways. My refuge there was in the basement, in a room with no windows and hard floors, but there were showers there. Plus it was on the edge of Tartarus, a mere jog from The Healer.

A pang of trepidation rolled though me as I holstered my gun and filled my bag. I was breaking the system, but what choice did I have? Break the system or risk being exposed during the daylight? Neither was a great option, but one was more likely to end up with me dead. The two Ravagers today were nothing, a fluke, but to be on the streets, in the open… that would be a tempting fate.

I checked my watch. Darkness had fallen.

I released the magazine on my gun and checked the cartridge. It was still full. Setting the safety, I holstered it again and took a deep breath. Moving more carefully now, I crawled into the vent and headed out into the darkness. Tonight was a night I would steal my food or die trying.

3. RECKLESS

It was frustrating moving across the rooftops tonight. My leg ached every time I landed heavily on it causing me to limp the next few strides. But no matter how badly it hurt, I pushed through it. There wasn't time to complain or feel sorry for myself, the only thing I could do was work to fix it. No matter how bad the pain gets, you have to keep moving forward.

I could see the Ravager's reserve warehouse from nearly a mile away, the glass skylights illuminated in the dark night. I was never able to figure out how they had power while the rest of the city was constantly swallowed in blackness. While their dull humming lights weren't bright, they were still glowing. In all honesty, it almost put them at a disadvantage. As I stood in the dark, my well-adjusted eyes could see their every movement in the glowing lamps. But from their perspectives, they could barely see past the pools of light into the shadows beyond. With my black attire and cloaked hood I was nearly invisible.

Ravagers were violent, but not very bright.

Hunched, I wrapped my fingers over the edge of the building. Three guards moved lazily below me. I could see the sheen of black metal as they adjusted their guns. Even with all of the advances in technology, guns had still proven to be one of the most efficient and inexpensive ways to kill someone at a long distance. Things like chemical warfare risked too many lives, proving hard to contain and weapons of mass destruction weren't such a great idea now that we were quarantined to such a small land mass. Most other modern day weapons would debilitate your target, slow them down, or render them unconscious. But here in Tartarus we aimed to kill. Knives and guns have been killing successfully for thousands of years, so why change a good thing. If anything, modern technology has only improved upon an already successful weapon. There were bullets that could track body heat, scopes that could see up to ten miles and knives that produced an electrical shock strong enough to singe your internal organs. Fortunately for me, these kinds of weapons were rare outside of The Wall.

I waited until the guards passed to make their rounds and lifted the makeshift ladder I had stashed on the rooftop. The span between the two roofs was too big to jump, but a well-placed ladder made a decent bridge. The wood landed lightly on the other side and I began to move steadily across before they returned. The wood creaked and shifted slightly under my weight but I moved onward unfazed. I always figured if it broke I would fall and die. Better it was at the hands of gravity while I tried to survive than in the grip of a Tribe while I surrendered.

The tarred rooftop was still warm from the day's sun, my shoes sticking slightly to the surface. I moved with ease to the second glowing skylight on the left. The third pane lifted with ease, letting a blast of warm air out.

My mouth watered as the sweet smell of food swirled around my face. They must have gotten fresh supplies today; I could smell bread mixed in the grainy scented air. What I would give to taste that freshly baked bread… but unfortunately food like that was not worth the risk of getting caught. MREs and canned supplies were the safest choice. They were always pushed on the back shelves, temporarily forgotten. Even procuring The Healer's herbs was a risk I rarely took, but the fire burning in my shin made it a necessity tonight.

Removing my backpack, I concealed it in a nearby air duct and pulled out my tote. With calculated movements, I slid through the open pane and transitioned expertly to the exposed beams. Careful to keep my feet centered, I focused on the next support beam and moved forward.

The key was not to look down.

The dropoff was nearly forty feet, but if I kept my eyes focused on the goal my feet remained steady. I continued this choreographed dance of sorts for another three beams until I reached the old water supply pipe running from the roof. Keeping to the shadows, I used the connecter pipes as steps and descended into the belly of the warehouse.

Most of the guards remained outside, confident no one could infiltrate their watch. The few guards inside took little notice of anything around them. From the looks of it two of them were nearly fornicating in the corner, while a third proceeded to stuff his face with some kind of meat. The bullring in his nose pressed against the meat with each bite as red juices dripped down his lips, collecting in his exposed chest hair. I had to look away to keep from gagging.

All three bore the marks of their Tribe. Black clothing marked with red, piercings covering their extremities. The woman's long black hair was shaved on the sides before cascading into a waist length ponytail. Beauty was not something the Ravagers held in high esteem. The harder you looked, the more respect you got.

With the three of them effectively distracted, I continued on my hunt. Keeping pressed to the back wall, I scanned the shelves for what I needed. I knew the herbs were closer to the guards and decided it would be easier to get those without a full bag.

Careful not to bump up against the tightly packed shelving, I wove my way forward in a crouch. People's eyes naturally searched at the average human height level, the key was to either stay low or move up high.

The herbs were only three rows ahead of me, but the sex driven couple was on the move. I dropped to my belly behind a sack of potatoes just as her steel toed boots passed.

"Don't you walk away from me!" The man growled as he pursued her.

She turned flipping him a rude hand gesture. "You don't own me."

"Like hell I don't," his hand flashed out, winding in her ponytail as he yanked violently backwards. Her heels clattered on the floor as she toppled backwards grabbing at his hand. Catching her by the throat, he smashed his face to hers claiming her lips as she struggled. Then, with a startled cry, he dropped her. His blood smeared her lips as she grinned up at him. Cackling like a hyena she spit his lip ring back at him.

I thought he was going to kill her, but to my disgust he grinned and climbed on top of her instead.

As they pawed hungrily at each other, I crawled forward, desperate to get away.

With the two of them now engaged in the middle of my path, I had to take a longer route. Fortunately the herbs were right where I expected them to be. There were some I recognized like ginger root, garlic and rosemary. Those I didn't, I knew The Healer would. Careful to take enough for a trade, but not so much that their loss would be noticed, I filled a third of my bag.

In case the lovers where still disgustingly engaged, I moved further away and headed for the back wall. Something rotten filled my nose. Turning, my blood began to boil. Standing before me was racking filled with rotting food.

People were starving, scraping for scraps and these animals had enough food to let it rot.

My hands shook with anger.

Another cackle from the woman reminded me I should keep moving. With less restraint I began grabbing something off every shelf I passed, filling my bag. As my fingers nimbly worked their way up the pipe and my leg screamed in pain, I smiled. The heavy bag resting against my back felt vindicating. After carefully replacing the glass pane and hiding my ladder, I took off at a steady pace to find The Healer.

It was fortunate that her hideout was so close to the Ravagers' warehouse. After all of the physical activity I could feel the blood beginning to seep through my makeshift bandage. The Healer's hut was an old abandoned water tower on the city limits. She had broken off the ladder at some point, creating an unreachable tower. Even a skilled climber as myself could not make it up the entire way without falling.

Upon reaching the base of her tower I leaned against the huge support leg. My fingers searched, quickly finding the rusted hole I sought. Leaning close I whistled a three-pitch tone. A minute later, a hatch opened. I stood perfectly still. I knew at that moment a gun was pointed at my head. If I moved too fast or appeared to be a threat, she would shoot me. I must have passed her test because eventually a rope ladder dropped from the tower. Checking my gun and knife one more time, I then climbed upward towards The Healer.

The air was stifling as I emerged into the round metal room. A heavy smoke clung to the air, a faint scent of rot lingering on it. The room was nearly as dark as the night outside, except for the small fire burning in the center of it.

"Don' ya dally girl." A rough voice spoke in broken English from the shadows. "Pull up da rope."

My skin crawled as it did every time I came in contact with The Healer. I hated pulling the rope ladder up and trapping myself in this metal dome with her. As much as I detested it, trading with her meant playing by her rules and I needed those antibiotics.

Her faded eyes scanned my bag as I closed the hatch. "Whatcha go' for me today?"

Without saying a word I pulled the tote from my bag and dumped its contents out on her table. My portion of the food was already carefully stowed at the bottom of my bag.

23

Her eyes widened as they took in my offerings. "Ya mus' be in need of sometin big. An from ya limpin I say 'is ya leg."

"I need some of your antibiotic salve, preferably a double batch this time." My hand rested on the holster as I waited for her response.

"We may 'ave a deal." She began moving about the room gathering things in her withered hands. "Set ya self on the table an let da Healer look."

Keeping my eyes on her, I carefully sat upon her cluttered table avoiding what looked like entrails. Dropping a pile of jars and rags next to me she yanked up my pant leg with surprising speed for an old woman. My fingers reflexively twitched toward the hilt of my knife.

Clucking her tongue, she peeled back my bandage, pulling some of the scabbing skin with it. I sucked in a sharp breath.

"Dangerous world deez days." She muttered before smearing some rotten smelling cream over the raw skin. While the stench burned my nose, the pain in my shin was almost instantly relieved. I sighed with pleasure.

She grinned a gapped smile at me. "See da ol' Healer knows."

Her hands wound a new bandage over my leg, and then began collecting the jars intended for me. "Leave dat on for thirty time, den apply dis."

I pulled my pants over my leg and took the jars from her, placing them in my now nearly empty sack. With impressive strength she pulled open the hatch and kicked the ladder down.

Before descending I tossed her one of the romance novels. "For your troubles."

She grinned, "I see ya soon, I sure."

Hastily, I retreated down the ladder. The second my hands were free of the rough rope it rose back into the hatch. I took a deep breath of fresh air as I watched the hatch close. We both got something of benefit and no one died. It was a good trade. With my feet back on solid ground, the medicines clinking in my bag and the hatch door closed, I finally took my hand off my gun.

Without looking back I headed for the nearest building, knowing the back corner's drainpipe was still intact.

My leg felt amazing as I sat on the edge of the rooftop. The searing pain was nothing more than a dull ache now. While The Healer was not my favorite merchant, she definitely knew her stuff. Casually, I leaned back against the behemoth gargoyle perched on the side of the building, letting my feet dangle precariously over the edge. The sky tonight was clear; even a few stars could be seen through the atmospheric haze. I checked my pocket watch. There were still two hours until sunrise and I could easily be at the school within twenty minutes.

I picked up a piece of rubble and chucked it into the open space before me. As always my curiosity sparked as I watched the sky crackle and pop when the rock collided with the invisible force field. While the city of The Sanctuary was protected within the great iron walls that stood as high as most buildings, there was also some kind of force field above that. I used to think about jumping off a building to try and clear the metal walls below, but after witnessing a bird fly into the force field, that thought quickly died. The invisible electrified fence shocked the poor creature, sending its charred remains plummeting back towards the earth. The Wall wasn't merely a man-made barricade, but an impenetrable force field whose heights knew no bounds. On the rare occasion I was close enough to it, the temptation to fling things at The Wall was irrepressible.

There was little else beyond what was our city. Outside the masses of buildings was just dead, open land. There were broken stretches of streets filled with the skeletons of motor vehicles, but even those didn't lead anywhere anymore. There was nothing left to lead to. What wasn't wasteland was toxic water and what wasn't toxic water was wasteland. Even Tartarus was a mere fleck of its former self. What was once a prosperous city was now just blackened streets and broken buildings. The choices weren't great. You could escape the Tribes and die of exposure or deal with the Tribes in the urban jungle that was once a city and stand a chance— however small— at surviving.

I pinched another piece of rubble in my fingers, ready to fling it when a commotion erupted in the streets beneath me.

Shouting echoed off the abandoned buildings, bouncing back at me from all angles. There was a sound of distant gunfire as I rose to my feet, followed by the Ravager hunting cry. They were tracking someone. That eerie cry meant one thing and one thing only— someone was going to die tonight.

I hopped back over the ledge to the rooftop, it certainly would not be *my* blood spilled tonight. Another cry pierced the night and I reflexively turned in its direction. I could see the Ravagers' torch lights glowing in the distance. From the sound of it, they were closing in on their prey. I squinted as something moved thirty feet in front of them in the shadows. How strange that they should be hunting at night.

As the thought crossed my mind, the tiny shadow moved into the light from the street lamps. My heart dropped.

She was only a child.

Even from this distance I could see her body shaking with fear. Her long mousy hair clung to the small cherubic face as she searched for an escape. Panic filled me as I watched her frozen frame.

"Run!" I muttered to her under my breath.

Another gunshot fired, the bullet sparking as it struck the lamppost next to her. Falling backwards she scrambled away darting down the nearest alley. My gut clenched. I knew that alley, I knew *every* alley, and she had just trapped herself in a dead-end.

The Ravagers knew it too. Slowing their pace, they

sauntered to the mouth of the alley, cat-calling at the little girl.

"*Run away.*" My mind told me. "*Leave her, this doesn't affect you.*"

While I agreed with this callous voice of reason, my body was already in motion. My feet carrying me to the edge of the roof, I blindly dove for the next building, bounding forward when my feet connected. Just one more rooftop and I would be upon her. I sprinted for the back corner of the building where I knew there was a half-constructed drainpipe. It was missing the last fifteen feet to prevent someone from climbing up it. But the drop could be managed with a calculated fall.

Moving like a shadow, I flipped my body over the side of the building and flung myself downward. My feet slid on the metal, finding purchase just before the pipe abruptly cut off. Scanning the dark alley I caught a glimpse of movement behind an overturned dumpster. She was only about ten feet in front of me. I began calculating my jump as the first leather clad hunter appeared at the mouth of the alley. He was idly twirling a bat as his side. Various spikes protruded from the head like lethal thorns.

"Maaaarrrrrco…" He called mockingly from the end of the alley. Rolling laughter erupted behind him as pierced bodies filled the narrow opening. There were about fifteen of them, the glinting metal and shaved heads making it nearly impossible to delineate the men from the women. But from my vantage point, it looked like the hunting pack was mostly male. My stomach churned.

Escape or die. Getting caught was not an option.

The leader took a few calculated steps down the alley, dragging the spikes against the ground as he moved.

"You're supposed to say 'Polo' little one or don't you want to play with us?" The girl huddled further against the wall. "Don't worry, we'll be gentle…"

The knife left my hand as the bloodthirsty crowd exploded with mirth. The blade flickered for an instant in the darkness before burying itself into the leader's left eye. The

27

ensuing chaos was instantaneous.

The horde continued to laugh for several heartbeats before their leader's screams reached their ears. When his massive body hit the ground, writhing as he clung to the handle protruding from his eye socket I leapt toward the ground. Calculating the fall, I landed lithely on my feet letting the momentum roll my body forward. But I had underestimated the force of my fall. I rolled out into the center of the alley, stopping in a low crouch as fourteen and a half sets of eyes fell upon me. My gun was drawn and firing before they could react. Darting to the side I ducked behind the dumpster as bullets began to rain down on us. Based on the screams I had hit a few more of the heathens. At least if I was going down I would take a few of the scum with me. A tiny hand grabbed my arm and I turned to meet two terrified brown eyes. I gritted my teeth. She was no older than I was when I was left alone in this city.

Grabbing her petite body I pressed it into mine, shielding her from the onslaught of debris. The bullets were beginning to eat through the rusted metal. It wouldn't be much longer before they could reach us. It took my ringing ears a second to realize the gunfire had ceased.

Someone was still screaming in pain.

"If you give us the girl, we might just let you live." A female's voice called this time.

The child began to shake in my arms again.

"Leave and you may not need an eye patch like your friend." I called in a calm voice back to her. It was a farce, my only knife was gone and by my count there were only three bullets left in my gun.

"You had better hope this bullet finds you first princess, I won't be so gentle." The woman's voice echoed back.

There was an odd, high-pitched humming coming from the mouth of the alley. Without hesitating I yanked the girl off the ground and ran for the corner where the drainpipe was. If I lifted her high enough there was a ledge barely big enough for a child to stand on, from there she could reach the pipe. At least she could escape.

"You have to climb!" I screamed at her as I thrust her into the air. I felt her tiny feet scramble as her hands found their grip. The humming was getting louder, the tone nearly unbearable. The sound stopped just as she left my hands and my back exploded into shreds of fire where the heat-seeking bullet found me.

I slammed against the wall before staggering backwards, but as I fell there was a second explosion from somewhere behind me. This was not the work of a gun. A brilliant white light swallowed the alley, searing my retinas. I blinked— at least I thought I blinked. It felt like my eyes were open, but I saw nothing. I heard nothing.

I fell at an old angle, my limbs feeling disjointed from my body. Nothing moved, even my chest stilled as the pain seeped through my body.

This was it.

Hands found me, tugging and pulling at my limp body. The Scavengers were already upon me, stealing what little I had left in this world.

A small part of me found peace. So this is how it happens, this is how I die. All of those years of wondering and now I knew...

4. LOST

Death was not as I had expected it to be. I thought I would drift away, become nothing, and finally get the rest I never had in my damned existence called a life. Instead it smelled funny, like chemicals. And as time pressed on, awareness of my body came back to me. There was no pain, no sight, no sounds. I just felt like a useless body drifting in a sea of nothingness.

I hated it.

When my hearing began to return, I was actually pleased to realize I wasn't dead. The shock of that realization surprised me. For so long I thought about death and now that I was so close it, I was actually relieved I had eluded it. How strange...

At first there was just a ringing sound. Then, as the ringing slowly faded, voices started to emerge from the silence. I couldn't understand them at first, but eventually the murmurs started to sound like words. There was one voice I seemed to hear the most. It spoke frequently, in long intervals, its deep rumblings oddly comforting. While the words were often fuzzy, it took me a while to realize he was reading to me.

I drifted from consciousness, my dreams and reality

melding together. Time was lost to me. My body refused to respond and my sight was yet to return. I felt no pain, but I also felt no sense of being. I began to pray for those moments when the heavy voice would read to me and allow me to escape my own mind.

Then one day, the light in my eyes flickered on. Like my hearing, my vision trickled back slowly, first seeing lights, then colors, then finally making out tiles and shoes. I was lying on my stomach, my face planted in some kind of open support. I slowly began to match shoes with voices.

The day my toes and fingers started tingling with feeling again, a new pair of beige linen shoes stepped into my line of sight.

"I know that you can hear me and I am going to keep this brief." The female's voice was monotone, bordering on cold. "Your body has been kept in a state of suspended animation to allow for maximum regeneration. Soon, you should be regaining feeling in your extremities, if you're not already. As a courtesy, you should know you are currently under armed guard. So I suggest remaining calm and peaceful when you completely awaken."

The shoes disappeared from sight and my ears became keenly aware of two different sets of breath somewhere nearby.

My mind raced, looking for an answer as to where I was. For reasons unknown to me, my captors had not only prolonged my life, but saved it. I was not with the Ravagers, that was certain. There was a possibility I could be with the intellectual Adroits, but Tribes generally never cared about the lives outside of their own circles.

I thought of the young girl I had pushed to safety. She had reached the ledge, of that much I was sure. I could remember the feeling of her tiny legs wiggling upward from my grasp. Beyond that though, her fate was unknown to me.

I hoped the utter stupidity of my sacrifice hadn't been for nothing.

In all honesty, I couldn't say what made me go to her.

31

Or what made me break all of my rules and stick my neck out for another human being. It was a stupid and self-destructive action. But there was no use in regretting it now. I chose my path, executed my actions and now there were consequences to be dealt with. Dwelling in the past would get me nowhere; instead I needed to focus on the situation at hand. Now that I wasn't dead, surviving was once again the key game.

The curt woman had been right. Feeling slowly began to seep back into my body. As I cautiously flexed my tingling fingers, the sound of hands readjusting on triggers answered me. There was a beep and a voice nearby spoke.

"She's moving."

There was no response, no movement within the room, but the tension in the air was palpable. Moving with great care I lifted my hands holding my palms up as a sign of amenability. When no one shot, I placed them beneath my chest and pushed myself upwards just enough to raise my head.

I blinked at the room, finding it dingier than I had expected. The lights glowing above me gave off a familiar green hue. Instead of finding sterile white tile on the walls as I had expected, they were concrete. Large cabinets layered them, covering most of the space. There were no windows.

I swallowed.

One of the guards moved, catching my attention. He was wearing dull-colored clothing and looked nothing like any of the Tribesman I had ever seen. His blonde hair was long, pulled back in a ponytail. His hand reflexively tightened on his gun as I looked at him. He watched me warily, as if I would suddenly fly off the table and attack at any moment. Someone else in the room moved and I turned to see another soldier pushing back a tall, thin man with glasses. I was surprised when he glared at the guard.

"Don't be foolish Doc." The dark-haired soldier spat at the tall man.

"Don't be such a brute and learn some compassion. She's a human being, not a rabid animal." With a force I was surprised such a lanky man could possess, he shouldered the guard out of the way. In his hands was a pile of clothing.

Looking down, I immediately lowered myself further on the table and pulled my arms around my bare chest.

The so-called doctor laid the clothing next to me and pulled up a sheet to shield my body from the guards. Just looking at the pile I knew the clothing would be too big, but that was the least of my problems. While hastily pulling on the faded grey shirt and black linen pants, I glared at the dark haired man with the gun.

His returning gaze made my skin crawl.

Once my body was covered, the doctor dropped the cloth and stepped back. He looked young, younger than I would have envisioned a doctor being. Fidgeting under my steady gaze, he removed his glasses, wiping them on his shirt as he cleared his throat.

"My n-name is Porters. I'm the resident doctor and have been tending to your injuries. If it is alright with you I would like to touch you to take your vitals." His hands twisted nervously.

The black-haired guard's finger pressed over his trigger, but he did not yet point the barrel at me. The blonde guard's gaze flickered to his colleague, looking for guidance.

They were afraid of me.

I tried not to smile as the thought crossed my mind. Although I was unarmed and half their size, I sparked fear in these men. Even the leering guard in the corner showed a hint of fear behind his imperious eyes.

I nodded once at the man named Porters.

He moved slowly, touching his fingertips to my wrists, flashing a light in my eyes and feeling my neck and shoulder. I was careful to keep my eyes on his face, but my focus was actually on the dark-haired guard. His black eyes were focused intently on me.

Trusting your instincts in Tartarus could save your life and that man made my scalp prickle. He would prove to be an adversary. I could feel it in my bones.

Porters stepped away from me looking pleased. "Everything looks good. Your back has healed nicely, your heart rate is strong and your retinas have reattached perfectly."

I nodded my head again, acknowledging the information. I remembered the hum as the heat-seeking gun charged, the fire as the bullet pierced my skin. Then there was an explosion. I couldn't remember what had caused it though, just the blinding light and force as it blew me backwards.

Before he could utter another word the doors opened and a woman walked in flanked by two other armed men. She had stark white hair that was pulled back into a severe bun. The grey suit that loosely fitted her lean body only accented her pale features further. Her face was long and thin with a sharply pointed chin. Despite the color of her hair, her face was relatively un-aged. There were two faint lines at the corners of her eyes hinting at passed years, but I would have guessed she was probably in her forties. Close to what my own parents would now be if they were still alive. Her brilliant honey-toned eyes fell immediately upon me, but there was no look of maternal instinct or pity in them. I doubted this woman would prove to be an ally.

Her shoes caught my attention. They were the same beige pair I had seen not long ago. This was the cool-voiced woman. Confirming my observations, she began to speak.

"You are currently being held within the confines of my walls, against my better judgment. I will not waste my time on you, so you will answer my questions and you will be honest. If I believe you are deceiving me, I will have you shot on the spot. Do you understand?" Her tone was clipped.

I nodded, refusing to speak.

"Good." Her eyes narrowed. "What is your name?"

I didn't respond at first, narrowing my eyes. Immediately four guns pointed at my heart.

"Phoenix." I said, my voice sounding surprisingly strong.

She raised her hand and the guns lowered in response.

"What Tribe are you from?" She scrutinized my every movement.

"I don't claim allegiance to any Tribe."

"Fine, then what Tribe were you *born* to?"

"I wasn't *born* to any Tribe." The thought disgusted me. "I was born in The Sanctuary."

Her eyes tighten as she considered me.

"Take her to the cells." And with those last words she disappeared back through the doors.

Fury flared within me. I had answered all her stupid questions and now she was throwing me in a cage? I hadn't even gotten answers in return.

The sullen guard grabbed my arm and yanked me from the table. I stumbled against him, my legs weak from lack of use. Gathering myself, I pulled away, but his grip held tight. The cruel smile on his lips grew as he towered over me.

Porters laid a hand on him, his tone tense. "Go easy on her Maddox, she is not completely done healing yet."

Maddox snarled at the doctor. "Mind your business Doc. You healed her enough, now it is time to do my job."

I noticed how the doctor's eyes flickered from mine to Maddox's. Releasing the brute's shoulder, he stepped back and squared himself, drawing himself up to full height.

"It is your job to guard, but it is mine to protect. If anything happens to my patient under your watch, it will be your head I will come for." His face softened as he turned to me. "You need to drink a lot of fluids over the next few days. I will come and check on you *regularly*." His eyes darted to Maddox's on the last word.

The grip on my right arm eased slightly, but his pressure remained firm. Without another word to the doctor, Maddox dragged me from the room. The other guard appeared at my other shoulder as we moved through the door, but unlike his counterpart, he did not touch me.

They moved me at a quick pace, my usually agile feet

stumbling to keep up. The walls here were also concrete, showing no sign of weakness or escape. Every twenty feet or so the tunnels would split off creating new paths, but the receding hallways all looked the same to me. Naturally, my eyes darted around for any possibility of evasion or improvised weapons, but the hall yielded nothing. The smooth walls were clean and seamless. Every hallway was empty as we moved. I saw not a single other person.

My chances of escape were growing thinner.

We turned left and arrived at a completely open doorway with a panel next to it. The ponytailed guard pressed his palm to it. When the responding beep sounded, I was thrown unceremoniously inside. Maddox laughed pitilessly as I fell, sliding across the hard floor.

"Sweet dreams." He crooned winking at me.

It took every bit of self-control I had not to throw myself at him and begin clawing at his face.

The door beeped again and they left me unguarded. I stared at the open doorway shocked.

It couldn't be this easy.

Climbing to my feet I moved towards the door. I could see clearly into the hallway.

It was empty.

Stretching out my hand, I reached towards the door, then jumped.

"I wouldn't do that if I were you."

The voice came from the dark corner of the room. A boy about my age emerged from the shadows. He was thin, with jet-black hair that was cut closely to his head. Beneath his maroon shirt, tattoos covered his pale skin. I swallowed thickly as his brown eyes watched me.

He was a Taciturn.

Even had he not been wearing the color of his tribe— which he so obviously was— the tattoos were a dead giveaway. The Taciturns literally wore their pride on their skin. Their tattoos told of their past kills, personal triumphs or private vendettas. While the boy did not bear many markings, the ink was still prominent against his fair skin.

I glared at the thin boy and reached my fingers out further. Hell would freeze over before I would willingly stay in a room alone with a Tribesman.

The air crackled as my fingertips grew nearer to the doorframe. Before I could think to pull my hand away, sparks flew from my fingers and I was blown backwards. Everything faded to black before I even hit ground.

When I came to, I was lying on my back looking up into the face of the Taciturn boy. He smiled knowingly at me.

"I told you not to do that." His smile erupted into a full-blown grin as he offered me a hand. Glaring at his open fingers I rose, refusing his aid. He just shrugged and walked to an open cot on the other side of the room.

"Be thankful you only touched it with your fingertip. I pressed my whole palm to it. Came around three hours later and damn near soiled myself." He flung himself down on the cot and began picking at his cuticles.

Looking down at my own fingers, an angry burn was blossoming on my index finger. My brow furrowed. I turned my hand twice, staring at my nails. They were long, protruding grotesquely over my fingertips.

How long had I been unconscious?

I checked my other hand and then my arms before grabbing for my hair. Uncharacteristically it was pulled back. I pulled the tie holding it back and the greasy locks fell to below my shoulders. I gaped at the long blonde hair. I had always kept it short, cut blunt with my knife. The few times I ever caught my reflection I knew I looked too much like my mother. She was a beautiful woman, but in Tartarus beauty was a dangerous thing. It made you a lusted object, a target. It was a weakness and I hated it. Keeping it cropped short in a disheveled manner helped hide that attribute. I pulled at the hair, wishing it gone.

"Don't worry, you were only out for four days." A young man stood in the doorway watching me. His voice was oddly familiar.

He wore dark pants like the pair I had been given and a patched grey shirt that was frayed at the edges. There were no distinguishable Tribe markers on him. In his hands was a tray of food. Just as the guard had, he pressed his hand to the panel, waited for the beep then walked through the doorway. My new roommate bounded toward him, snagging a steaming bowl and chunk of something brown.

"About time, I was starving in here." He muttered, stuffing the chunk in his mouth.

The newcomer set the tray on what I assumed was to be my bed. I was surprised when he actually turned his back to me to do so.

Rule number one: trust no one.

Rule number two: never turn your back to someone. (See rule number one.)

I watched him with cautious eyes as he turned back to me. His face was startlingly gentle as he looked at me. His features were sharp, but those eyes were... There was something in those hazel eyes I barely recognized. Something I hadn't seen in a long time. Kindness?

"The regenerating serum does that." He gestured to my hair and nails. "It enhances cell growth. Doc Porters is fascinated by it, he used it to heal your back. One of the side effects, however, is that your other more influential cells, like hair and nails, grow at an accelerated rate as well."

I stared at him, unable to find anything to say.

"I will be back for the dishes later. The water is for you. Doc Porters said you needed to keep hydrated." Looking me over one more time he turned to leave. As he pressed his hand to the panel I found my words.

"Thank you."

He stopped in the doorway, but did not turn around. "You're welcome."

I watched as he disappeared around the corner.

"So she speaks." My cellmate eyed me over his soup

bowl.

"Aren't Taciturns supposed to be the strong silent type?" I let a little venom slide into my words as I moved to inspect the food left for me.

"Not all of us fit the molds we were born into." His gaze hardened.

I cautiously sniffed the soup, my stomach awakening in response. It smelled delicious and there was steam rising from its surface. I couldn't remember the last time I had eaten something hot. Reason told me my captors would not waste their time rescuing me, just to poison my food. But I still struggled with the idea of eating something I had not prepared.

"If you're not going to eat that I will." The Taciturn boy called.

I wanted the will power to give him my food and see if it killed him, but I was too hungry. Instead I compromised, tossing him the brown chunk I supposed was bread and sipped at my soup.

He caught the bread with ease and stuffed it into his mouth. "Cheers."

I watched him as I finished my bowl and then drained my water glass.

"So why are you here, Taciturn?" We watched each other cautiously from our respective cots.

"I left my Tribe due to… artistic differences. As I'm sure you know, leaving a Tribe isn't the easiest thing. I was jumped by my own and left for the Scavengers to feed on. Three days later I woke up here." He gestured to the room around us.

"And where exactly *is* here, Taciturn?" I began biting my nails back down to a reasonable length.

"No idea. Unfortunately our captors are better with the questions than the answers." He shoved another hunk of bread in his mouth. "It's Arden by the way, I despise being referred to as *Taciturn*."

I wondered if that was his real name. Regardless, this

forsaken Tribesman may prove to be a good source of information if not an ally. And right now I needed as many allies as I could get.

"Phoenix." I offered as a sign of camaraderie.

He smiled around the hunk of food in his mouth, taking my bait. Before I could ask any more questions the room was cast into darkness as the light went out. I jumped to my feet ready for an attack. I could see Arden's eyes glinting in the darkness.

"Easy Phoenix, it's just lights out. They'll rudely wake us in the morning with them again when they want us up. No point wasting a good night's sleep." The springs of his cot squeaked as he settled in for the night. "I *am* a light sleeper though, so don't try anything stupid."

With his warning still ripe in my ears he rolled over and almost instantly began snoring. I had never before slept in the same room as another person and his presence left me feeling twitchy in the dark. Worse than knowing someone else was in the room with me was knowing there was a door *I* could not pass through but anyone else could easily walk in. My mind instantly thought of the dark-haired guard, Maddox, and his overtly roaming eyes.

I curled up in the middle of my cot and pulled my knees to my chest. Rigidly, I pressed my back against the concrete wall and braced myself for a long night. From my vantage point I could see both the doorway and Arden's slumbering form.

If anyone was coming for me tonight, I would know.

***

I started awake with a jolt; the familiar scream caught in my throat as it did every morning. At some point in the night I could no longer fight my body's exhaustion and I had fallen asleep. Choking back the scream I shook myself awake. How could I have been so stupid?

40

The room was still dark. Arden's motionless form was still breathing deeply but something had changed. The blanket I had left sitting at the foot of my bed was now draped over me. Our food tray was gone and a fresh glass of water lay on the floor by my cot. Someone had been in the room and I had slept thorough it. The hair on my arms stood up.

Normally I was so vigilant, so aware of my surroundings, and last night someone had not only come into the room without my knowing, but had actually managed to place a blanket on me without my knowledge. I shuddered and pushed the blanket away from me. Staring at the matte wool, I wondered if it was a sign of kindness or a threat, warning how close they could get to me.

In my experience, kindness did not exist in Tartarus.

The lights flicked on, causing me to flinch. Arden began to stir, grumbling as he folded his arm over his eyes. Not two seconds later the guards were outside our door scanning their palms to enter.

"Sleep well?" Maddox's hard eyes raked over me as he entered the room.

At the sound of his voice Arden jumped up from his bunk, clearly on edge.

"You two have a busy day ahead of you." It was the blonde ponytail that spoke this time. I had still not learned his name. Not that it really mattered. To my disappointment he moved toward Arden while the hulking Maddox descended upon me.

I restrained myself from breaking his nose when he grabbed my arm and yanked me from the cot. But the satisfied sneer on his face told me he could see the anger burning inside me. He was enjoying this.

They dragged us from our confines and at the first split in the barren hallways they separated us. I glanced over my shoulder. Arden was watching me too with apprehension in his chocolate eyes. Not wanting to appear weak, I broke our connection and marched forward with robotic precision.

41

Whatever torture they would administer, I would not give them the satisfaction of breaking me.

5. FOUND

The dark grey room had become painfully familiar over the last few days. Each fissure in the wall, every stain descending from the ceiling, I knew them all. I had prepared myself for the cruelest physical pain, but this monotony was almost worse.

I knew how to control myself, to play along. My first two outbursts in this room had earned me a taser gun in the ribs. Both times I woke up back in the cell with Arden staring down at me. After that, I realized their immediate intention was not to kill me, but they weren't about to set me free either. Every day I asked them questions as I answered theirs, but my queries were never answered. I was no further now than I had been the day I woke up in the doctor's office. My few belongings were still gone and the little girl's situation was still unknown. Arden, while a decent companion, proved equally useless, knowing less than I did about the city itself or our whereabouts.

As I stared at the greying walls for what felt like the hundredth time, I could feel my composure slipping.

"Where were you born?" The sandy-haired inquisitor asked me for the hundredth time.

I ground my back teeth together. "I have told you that already."

"Tell me again." His piercing eyes bore into mine.

"I was born in The Sanctuary. No, I don't belong to a Tribe. Yes, I survived on my own. NO, there is no one else I am working with. And NO, I don't know anything about The Sanctuary. I have no family, as I have said before they're all *dead*. AND NO, I have NO idea how the hell I got into this pit you call a city!" My voice rose with each sentence until I was nearly screaming. "I'm not answering any more of your idiotic questions until you answer some of mine!"

I jumped up from my seat and grabbed the edge of the table. With a force that surprised even myself, I jerked the table into the air and then slammed it to the floor. Papers splayed everywhere as the glasses of water exploded on the concrete floor.

The reaction in the room was instantaneous. The inquisitor jumped backwards pressing himself into the wall while Maddox's hands wound around my neck. I flailed, clawing at his arms as he yanked me off the ground. His grip tightened, making black spots appear in the corners of my vision. I had lost control. I knew that, but I didn't care. *Do it*, I thought, *go ahead and kill me*. It would be better than reliving this same day over and over again.

The door to the tiny room exploded open as the white-haired woman burst in.

"ENOUGH!" She screamed over the chaos.

Instantly we all froze. Maddox's hands released me and I crumpled to the floor gasping for air.

"Get Veyron to take her to the showers. She smells like a Scavenger." Disgust was strong on her stern face, "Keep the boy busy, I want to see her in the cell *alone*."

With one last look of revulsion in my direction, she swept from the room. How long had she been watching us?

Maddox yanked me to my feet, half carrying, half dragging me down a new hallway. He threw me into a small room covered in bleached tile. There was a shelf piled with clothing in the corner and a showerhead mounted to the wall. He shut the door behind him as he entered and I moved to further myself from him in the small space. Panic rose in my chest. I was trapped.

A hunger rose in his eyes as he gazed at me.

"You heard the boss, you smell like a repulsive rat." He gestured to the showerhead with his gun.

"She said for you to find another guard to take me here. I assumed Veyron would be a woman." Ice burned in my voice.

"Veyron has better things to do than babysit a defector like you. Besides, what's the matter little girl, embarrassed about your body? You know if you can't do it yourself, I will be forced to do it for you. And I won't be gentle." His dark eyes danced with pleasure as he attempted to intimidate me.

Suppressing the shudder running through me, I bit my cheek and began pulling off my shirt. I could have killed him, I wanted to. But the likelihood of my being able to disarm and subdue a man his size was not high. In an open space, where I had the chance to run, maybe. But trapped in this maze of never ending tunnels, I wouldn't get far. Besides, something in his eyes told me he would enjoy it if I fought back. That he might even lose control and force himself on me in the excitement. So instead of attacking him, I swallowed back the bile and continued to undress.

He leaned back against the wall, tapping his gun as a reminder of the power he held over me. His black eyes filled with lust as they raked over my exposed torso. The last thing I wanted was for this man to see me naked, but I wasn't going to give him the satisfaction of knowing I feared him. Going against all of my instincts, I turned my back to him. I tried to pretend he wasn't there, tried not to feel his eyes on me as I removed the rest of my clothing.

Keeping my back to him I turned on the water and stepped into the stream. It was freezing at first, but to my surprise the water warmed. Normally I would have taken my time—showers being such a rare thing and all—but Maddox's eyes were searing into my skin. I wanted nothing more than to put my clothes on again. I made sure to soap my stringy hair and wash the stench of captivity off my skin. As soon as the last of the suds slid off my body I snapped off the water and turned to face him. It took all of my strength not to cover my chest as his eyes traced my body.

"Not bad for a runt." He threw a towel in my face smirking as I covered myself. It was obvious he was aroused by the situation.

Using the towel as a shield I pulled new clothing from the pile and dressed hurriedly. I moved for the door and he clicked his tongue at me.

"Don't be leaving a mess for someone else to clean up after you. It's bad enough we have to feed you, we certainly aren't gonna be your maids too."

Quickly I gathered my strewn clothing and deposited them in the bin he indicated in the corner.

"See, not so hard, is it." To my relief he opened the door. This time as he grabbed my arm I couldn't repress my revulsion and I flinched away.

I instantly regretted it.

His black eyes glinted as he purposefully pulled me closer and began dragging me down the hall again. I swallowed the blood pooling in my mouth. The inside of my cheek was raw where I had chewed through the soft skin to keep from screaming.

I hated this man.

To my surprise the cell wasn't empty when we arrived. The white-haired woman stood with her hands laced behind her back as we entered. Her gaze flitted from my wet hair to Maddox.

"Leave us." Her voice was cool and controlled.

"But mam—" Maddox argued.

"I am plenty capable of handling this girl and my guards will be right outside." Her honey eyes were cold despite their naturally warm tone. I smiled vindictively as he was put in his place.

He nodded once and removed himself with one last longing glance at me.

"You look like her you know."

I snapped my eyes back to the stern woman.

"I almost didn't see it at first, but now with your hair long you look like her."

"Who?" I narrowed my eyes.

"You're stubborn like her too. Your mother."

I staggered back a step, as if she had just pulled a weapon on me. "You have no idea who my mother was."

"On the contrary child, I knew her better than you did. She is the reason I am trapped in this god-forsaken city." Heat blazed in her eyes. "So forgive me that I don't trust her offspring either."

I choked on my words. How could this woman know anything about me, about my family? She had to be lying.

"Funny how things come full circle sometimes." She tilted her head, appraising me. "It has become apparent to me that you are not going to be cooperative."

"Why should I be when you have done nothing for me in return?" I spat back.

"We saved your life."

I scoffed. "For what? To keep me prisoner in this hellhole? To make me suffer by living a longer life in this shitty city? If you wanted to do me a favor you would have let me die."

"I had a feeling you might say that." She stepped aside and I noticed my bag sitting on the cot behind her.

I made a move to grab for it but she blocked me. "We have removed anything that could be deemed a weapon. If you are willing to cooperate then you may keep your belongings."

Crossing my arms I gauged her. "What about my questions?"

She took a calculated breath before answering me.

"Some things will be answered in time, *if* you uphold your end of the deal, but for now… WEAVER!"

A handsome young man appeared in the doorway. At first I didn't even see the small body that clung to his side. As soon as he pressed his hand to the panel and it beeped, the tiny frame dislodged herself from his side and ran to me. A host of different emotions tore though my body as I watched the small child crash into my side, shock being the most prevalent. I stood frozen as her tiny arms wrapped around my waist. She buried her face in my shirt before turning her large doe eyes upwards to mine. Tears shimmered on her cheeks, but the look on her face was pure joy.

Hesitantly my arms wrapped around her. She was alive… she was here…

"She refuses to speak to us and has proven nearly as difficult as you. I am hoping that by reuniting you two, you will begin to be a little more cooperative. My name is Arstid. If you decide there is something imperative that you have not yet shared with us, ask for me personally."

Arstid turned to leave, but paused at the door.

"Jutta only had one child I knew of, so I assume this is not your sister."

The blow of hearing my mother's name hit harder than I expected. I nodded.

"Then why did you risk your life for this child?"

I turned my gaze down at the girl in my arms. "I don't know… I guess… because no one else was going to."

The truth was I didn't really know what made me save her. Arstid raised a white eyebrow before turning to leave. The moment she was gone I pulled the child away from me and knelt to her level.

"They haven't hurt you, have they?"

Tears still glistened on her round cheeks, but she shook her head no. I pulled my sleeve down and wiped her face dry.

"Have they been treating you okay?"

She shrugged and nodded.

"And feeding you?"

She nodded again. I sighed with relief as I gazed at the little stranger who had come so unexpectedly into my life.

"How old are you?"

She held up ten fingers, looking at each of them in turn. My heart felt like it was splintering. She was younger than I had been, younger than any child alone should be in Tartarus. Once abandoned by their Tribes, most kids lived only days, rarely seeing five.

"Don't you have a family?"

At this her face turned down and her eyes began to fill with tears again. She shook her head. A part of me wanted to hug her, to comfort her, but I couldn't do it. I wasn't the nurturing type. I could barely stand myself, much less other people. But something in this little girl softened me.

"What's your name?"

She swallowed thickly and I noticed for the first time the scar across her throat. It was an old one, healed with time like the one on the back of my head. It ran from the base of her left ear to her collarbone.

"You can't speak can you?"

She shook her head again. The child was not stubborn, as Arstid had falsely accused. She was a mute. I looked her over carefully. Her nails were chewed down to bloody stumps and her body was small. Too small, like mine was, like a child that knew hunger all too well. She must have been an abandoned orphan, undoubtedly pushed out by a family of Scavengers. It was amazing she had made it this long. The girl began to fidget under my gaze.

"It's okay, we can figure out your name later." She smiled a little at this. "I'm Phoenix."

Her smile widened.

We were interrupted by the beep of the door. The same young man with the food tray came in.

"I see you found your friend." To my surprise he was talking to the child. She grinned up at him with admiration. I looked at him more carefully now. Could this child see something in him I could not? Maybe his actions had been purely out of kindness and not a threat as I had first thought.

He bent and handed her a piece of bread. She grabbed it and plopped onto my cot enjoying the treat. He offered me the other. I gazed at his hand for a second before taking it.

"Thank you," I murmured as he smiled warmly at me.

Now that I wasn't looking for signs of deception in his every movement, I realized he was actually good looking. His sandy hair fell into disarray around his face. The lines of his features were severe, accented by a long nose and squared jaw, but his face was surprisingly gentle. When he smiled, so did his hazel eyes.

I turned away, not wanting to notice anything more about him.

"How did you get stuck with food duty?" I asked, remembering Maddox's harsh comment about having to feed us.

He shrugged, "I volunteered."

That was not the response I had been expecting.

"It doesn't bother you to be so close to prisoners unarmed?" I raised an eyebrow at him, noticing his conspicuous lack of weaponry. Everyone here seemed to be armed, even the stern-faced Arstid had a knife carefully concealed on her thigh. Only someone with trained eyes would have noticed it.

"I choose not to carry a weapon most of the time, besides I don't believe all of our guests wish me harm." His eyes softened a little as he looked at me.

I stared at him. The child raised her hands and he handed her a bowl of soup.

"Even the most gentle people have a dark side you know." I was trying to warn him.

"I know," he said handing me the other bowl of soup. "It's how you control that darkness that defines you."

Without another word he left, leaving my mind reeling.

That night I actually laid down in my bed for the first time since I had arrived. Arden had reappeared just before lights out and seemed unsurprised by our new addition. He just raised his eyebrows then shook his head. As the lights went out, a small hand grabbed mine from beneath the cot. I had offered the child my bed, but she just grabbed a blanket and curled up beneath it. I smiled at her natural instinct of preservation. She was sheltered below me and if someone came in the night they would have to go through me to get her. It was something I would do.

As my hand hung over the side of the cot, she sought it out, her tiny fingers wrapping around mine. I couldn't understand why this child trusted me so much. All of the adults here still looked at me with trepidation, like I might turn on them at any moment. But the child looked at me with confidence, reverence even. No one had ever looked at me that way.

My mind whirled. Just over a week ago I never had to think of anyone but myself. I never questioned my actions or needed anyone else's help, but now... something was different. I was still too hard, too calloused, but something foreign stirred within me.

I didn't like it.

How had my world changed so dramatically in such a short period of time? Six years I had managed without needing anyone and now I felt... hollow. Arstid said she knew my mother, that she had followed her here, but that could be a lie. The kind-faced boy had caused me to question not only myself, but to also wonder if some humans were actually capable of kindness. Even as his kind features flickered across my mind, the dark vile eyes of the hulking guard Maddox crossed my thoughts. Reflexively my hands clenched into fists. I envisioned all of the ways I would kill him, if I got the chance. I wanted to watch him suffer for what he had done to me today.

The tiny hand twitched within mine as she fell asleep. The anger boiling to the surface immediately began to ebb as she stirred beneath me.

My life was changing, fast, and I wasn't entirely sure I could handle it.

6. STRINGS

"Aster?"

The tiny brown head shook back and forth as she watched Doc examine me.

"Maggs?"

She stuck her tongue out, wrinkling her nose. Doc ran his fingers over the scar hidden in my hair, with a perplexed look.

"Every wound healed perfectly except for that one." He sat back scratching his head. "Your memories are still intact, yes?"

"Yes. Well, everything from the last six years at least." I shrugged. "Lilly?"

The girl shook her head again.

"You mean to say you have no memory of your childhood?" Doc looked at me in surprise.

"Nope." He didn't need to know I had a few flashes of memory. It was better just to keep those to myself. As much as I liked Doc Porters, he was still working for the other team. And, until I knew exactly who the other team was, the more I played dumb, the better. I tried another name. "Anders?"

"That sounds like a boy's name." Arden piped in from

his cot.

"I agree." Doc said, jotting down something in his journal.

"Well I'm running out of ideas here. If you two don't have any helpful suggestions you can keep your mouths shut."

The little girl grinned as we quarreled. We had spent the last few hours trying to guess her name. Suddenly her eyes lit up and she tapped her chest.

"You have an idea?" I offered her my words.

She nodded. She tapped her chest and then pointed to me.

"You want my name?"

She shook her head. She tapped her chest again, held up her palm in the air and then pointed to me. My forehead creased as I stared helplessly at her.

"I think she wants a name *like* yours. Something a little less… conventional." Arden said.

She nodded bouncing where she sat. Doc stopped writing, his interest piqued.

"Okay…you want a *different* name. Let me think."

I had chosen my new name out of a necessity to start fresh. When my parents died in that alley so did their precious little girl. I was what rose from her ashes. Phoenix naturally seemed the most fitting choice for my new life.

"I didn't keep my given name either you know? I chose mine and I think it's your right to choose the one you want," I said, meeting her curious eyes. She nodded furiously.

I looked at the way her small hands fidgeted as she watched me. Her eyes flickered from my face to the ground, quick and nervous. She reminded me of a mouse. Her small delicate features, dishwater hair and soft brown eyes seemed to fit the description.

"Mouse?" I asked tentatively and for the first time since we started the name game, she smiled.

***

54

It had been three days since Mouse had been brought to me and she followed me wherever I went within my imprisonment. She never left my side. She even slept in the cell with me, fighting vehemently if they tried to remove her. Eventually they conceded and just left her with me on a permanent basis. During my questionings, she sat under the table listening to me repeat the same answers over and over again. I loathed the man questioning me, but I remained calmer now, as to not frighten Mouse. Every night she slept underneath my bed, her hand constantly creeping around the edge to touch my fingers. I always reached back, ensuring her tiny hand I was still here.

Tonight, as her hand disappeared under the frame again, I realized for the first time in my life I felt responsible for someone other than myself.

The thought shook me.

I was awoken in the middle of the night by the sound of metal scraping on concrete. Arden cursed as I sat up rapidly, startling him.

"Sorry," he muttered. "I dropped my pillow behind my cot and it got stuck."

He jerked the cot again and a white lumpy object fell to the floor. As he leaned over to snag it, my eyes widened. In the dull lights reflecting from the hallway I could see the glint of metal and familiar horizontal lines.

There was an air vent.

My bag was sitting on the floor by my cot, the food and weapons had been removed but I could always steal more. It would be easy to slip into the vent without being seen. Arden was always taken away first, I would have nearly five minutes before they would notice I was gone and—

Mouse stirred beneath me and my thoughts instantly stopped, then took another route.

She was small. I could easily guide her through the vents with me, but then what? What would we do once we made it outside? I had barely been able to keep myself alive and fed. How could I possibly provide for her too?

I could leave her here. Tell her I was coming back… lie to her.

I felt sick just thinking about it. But here she would have food and care. With me she would suffer like I had. Even though leaving Mouse here was the better choice for her, the responsible one, the idea of not being able to protect her myself appalled me.

Arden shoved his cot up against the wall again, covering the vent. This time Mouse awoke to the noise. Her fingers crept over the wool blanket searching for me. A lump caught in my throat as I grabbed her fragile fingers and lay back down.

"It's okay, I'm right here. I'm not going anywhere." But even as I said the words my eyes stared at the spot on the wall where I knew the vent was.

When I woke in the morning Arden was already gone and the kind-faced boy sat on Arden's cot watching me. It should have startled me, made me angry that he had gotten into the room without my knowledge, but it didn't. Mouse sat at his side chewing on something red. A book was cradled in her lap.

I watched her, wide-eyed.

Something flew at my face. I caught it reflexively. The taut shiny surface was smooth against my skin. My heart rose.

An apple.

I had not eaten one since I was a child. Another photo flash from the past.

"No bread today?" I tried to keep the joy from my face.

"I figured you would be tired of bread." He stretched, rising from the cot.

"What do you have there?" I asked Mouse, eyeing her book.

She grinned and held it up for me to see. It had words and pictures of people making hand gestures. I furrowed my brow.

"It's a book on sign language. Since Mouse can't speak

56

I thought it important that she be able to express herself." He smiled down at the little girl.

I opened my mouth to ask more about the book, but at that moment a new guard entered the door, a woman. She was short and lean, with long muscles tracing her bare arms. Her blonde hair was pulled back in a tight ponytail, the tips of it just reaching her waistline. I rose as she moved into the room, her blue eyes on Mouse.

"Are you ready to return to classes now?" Her voice was high and maternal. Mouse shrank away from the woman.

Immediately, I moved in response to Mouse's reaction. As I inserted myself between the newcomer and the child, the woman's hand reflexively moved to her gun. My muscles tensed ready for attack, but before the situation could escalate, the young man placed his hand over hers in a calming gesture.

"Veyron oversees most of the youth here. Mouse was attending classes before she was brought to you. We think it is important to educate our children. Veyron is one of the best guards we have. Mouse couldn't be in safer hands." His hazel eyes were steady, trying to reassure me.

I turned to Mouse, gauging her reaction. She looked frightened.

"Did they take you to classes to learn, to read?" I knelt to her level.

She nodded.

"I think you should go with them. It is very important that you have an education. Knowledge can only better a person." I kept my voice soft. Without my father's teachings I would have never made it as long as I did.

Mouse leapt to her feet and clung to my neck.

"Are you scared they won't bring you back here?"

Her tiny head nodded furiously.

A large hand passed over my arms, careful not to touch me, and fell lightly on her back.

"Mouse, I *promise* we will bring you back here. Have I ever lied to you before?" His deep voice was close to my ear.

Mouse raised her red-brimmed eyes to his and shook her head no, but her hands tightened on my shoulder.

"I will take good care of her until you get back." He soothed the child, brushing the tears from her cheeks.

She looked at me, fear still in her eyes. I understood her fear of losing me. The thought of the air vent still burned in my mind.

"I *promise* I will still be here when you get back. I won't leave you." Those were the words she needed to hear. Wiping the last of the tears from her face she released me. I watched as she took Veyron's hand. The guard's face was astonished as she looked at me, like she had just seen a Ravager show kindness. I wanted to wipe the look off her face for her. I may be calloused, but I was still human. I could be humane, if I tried.

When the little brown head turned to me just before they left, I smiled at her once more in encouragement. After she disappeared my smile wavered. The vent… Had I just lied to the only person who had ever shown me adoration in this horrific city?

Before I could overthink it, the young man moved to the door gesturing for me to follow. "Come on, we have work to do."

I raised my eyebrows at him. "Since when is sitting in the same room, answering the same damn questions over and over again work?"

A smile pulled at the corner of his lips. "No questions today. If you are going to stay here for a while, then you need to start pulling your weight. Besides I figured doing something physical outside of that tiny grey room might do you good."

I moved quickly after him now, eager to do anything other than sit in that room again. And eager to move away from the vent that was calling freedom to me. I had promised I would be here when Mouse returned. My escape could wait another day.

To my pleasant surprise there weren't other guards waiting for us in the hall. I rejoiced at the absence of those leering black eyes.

"No Maddox today?" I meant to sound casual, but there was too much spite in the way I said his name.

The sandy head turned at the harshness in my tone. "No, it's just you and me today."

A mild relief washed over me. If it came down to a fight I had a better chance defending myself against this man than the hulking Maddox. It was horrible to think, but it was true. I tried to focus on the sounds of our feet and not on the attack moves I could use on him that were flickering through my brain.

"Don't waste that. Apples are hard to come by these days." He eyed the perfect red fruit in my hand. I jumped at the opened conversation, needing a distraction.

"You never told me your name." I took a bite of my apple relishing in its juicy sweetness.

"You never asked."

That brought me up short.

"You have a point." I waited for him to respond but he continued forward in silence. I rolled my eyes at his stubborn back. "So what *is* your name?"

"Triven," he replied. While I could not see his face, I was sure he was smiling.

"Phoenix," I offered in return.

"I know." He was certainly smiling now.

We had moved down several halls I had not seen before. There were more doors, more sounds of other people. We stopped in front of an archway; there was no scanner panel here, just an open walkthrough. A pungent aroma filled the air around me as we moved through it, mixed with the foul stench of human filth. The room was ten times bigger than any I had seen so far. Blackened pipes hung from the ceiling above great vats. One side of the room was filled with piles of filthy rags and clothing. At the other end fresh linens hung from wires and piles of nicely folded clothing lay next to them.

"Work." Triven gestured to the piles around him.

"Every person here contributes in some way. Today we are going to help with the laundry."

The work was easy, mindless even, but it felt so good to be on my feet moving again that I didn't care. We worked mostly in silence; folding the dry garments, hanging the wet to dry and washing the dirty clean. It was systematic and we worked surprisingly well as a team, the large pile dwindling quickly.

"Are there usually others in here helping?" I asked, wiping the sweat from my brow.

Triven mirrored me, pressing his sleeve to his glistening temple. "Normally yes, but Arstid felt it was safer to keep you from the other citizens for now."

It surprised me to hear stern-faced Arstid had agreed to my little outing. But even more surprising was hearing Triven call his people citizens not Tribesman.

"Triven," I waited until his eyes met mine. "Where *are* we?"

I knew there was fear in my eyes and for the first time since I arrived here, I didn't try to hide it.

He leaned closer opening his mouth to speak, but a louder voice rang out. My muscles instantly tensed at the sound.

"That's enough work for today." Maddox's voice boomed in the large room. "Arstid has requested your presence."

The blood in my veins boiled as his eyes raked over my sweat-soaked body. I was now acutely aware of just how tightly my damp clothing clung to my skin.

"We can't have you appearing before her like that though. Showers first, I think..."

I actually recoiled as his meaty hand reached for me. It was a sign of weakness. I feared him and the horrid smile on his face proved he knew it. Hatred crept through me— hatred at myself for exposing my fear and hatred at him for delighting in it.

I braced myself to attack. I would die before I let that man defile me. He had managed to restrain himself from touching me last time, but the hunger in his eyes told me I might not be so fortunate again.

To my surprise, a body stepped between us, blocking me from Maddox's reach. Triven rose to his full height, but Maddox still towered over him.

"I will take her to the showers and then to see Arstid. You are dismissed." There was a harshness in Triven's voice I had never heard before. It was commanding and strong.

Despite the murderous look on Maddox's dark face, he backed down.

"Fine," he hissed though his teeth, but he didn't move.

Motioning with his hands, Triven guided me around Maddox's hulking frame, careful to keep his body between us at all times. I moved awkwardly, making sure not to turn my back to Maddox and fear prickled over my scalp when Triven did. His eyes were tense when they met mine, but he kept his unarmed back to Maddox. Still cautious not to touch me he motioned towards the door. My heart hitched as Maddox's hand twitched on his gun.

"It's okay, turn around and move. He won't follow us." Triven's words were only loud enough for me.

Every instinct I had screamed at me as I slowly obeyed. But as I moved skittishly toward the doors, only one set of footsteps followed. Once we cleared the doorway, Triven took lead again. I instantly felt better, no longer glancing over my shoulder. But that relief was short-lived. We were going to the showers. And while Triven's gesture seemed protective at the time, I now wondered if he had just challenged Maddox for the chance to leer at me himself. My stomach roiled as we grew near the shower area. Upon reaching the black door he opened it gesturing for me to enter first. My heart sank when he followed me inside letting the door click shut behind him. I gagged as my throat restricted, backing into the corner. But his eyes were not filled with the lust I had seen in Maddox's. A

61

wave of emotions rolled over his hazel eyes, but lust was not one of them. A few I did recognize, like pity, anger and pain.

He pointed to the pile of fresh clothing in the corner, unable to meet my eyes.

"There are fresh towels and clothing when you are done. Your old clothing can go in that bin and someone will retrieve it later for the laundry." He took a tentative step backwards. "I will be outside if you need anything."

Then he left.

I stood in shock as the door clicked shut again. At first I waited for him to come back in, to reappear coincidently just as I had undressed, but the door remained shut. I moved silently to the door staring at the handle. It didn't move.

There was a lock.

Quickly flipping it, I waited. Surely, as soon as the metal clicked into place the banging and shouting would ensue, ordering me to open the door. But as the bolt fell into place no shouts were issued. I took a deep breath and slouched against the wall in relief. For this brief moment it was as if I were free.

The shower felt wonderful this time with no eyes watching me, but even so, I did not linger too long. Locks were great and all, but keys still overruled them. As I pulled on the fresh clothing—for which I now had a newfound respect—I finally felt clean for the first time in months. Putting my dirty clothes in the black bin, I smoothed my hair and headed back to my captivity.

Triven was seated on the floor in the hallway. His hair was wet and a fresh shirt clung to his biceps. He smiled as I looked him over.

"I hope it's okay I decided to shower too. After I heard you bolt the door I figured it might be a while." He ran his fingers through his damp hair.

I blinked at him. He had left me alone and unguarded and was asking if it was okay? Did he really trust me not to run?

"You trusted me?" The thought escaped my mouth.

His returning smile was soft. "You promised Mouse

you would be there tonight when she returned. I knew you wouldn't disappoint her."

Shame overcame me. I had thought about it though. I had thought about leaving her here and never looking back. I was still thinking about it. But for tonight he was right, I wasn't ready to run just yet.

Humming quietly to himself, he led the way to Arstid's office. The doors to her quarters looked like any other, black aged metal fitted roughly into the cement walls. We stopped outside of the heavy door. Triven knocked three times before a voiced called us in.

Structurally, the room was the same as every other I had seen, but the furniture seemed oddly out of place. In the center of the room was an oversized round table. Surrounding it was an array of chairs in varying levels of shabbiness. No two were alike. There were bookcases of random sizes and colors, every shelf filled with books, artifacts and weapons. It looked like a furniture graveyard. This must not have been her office, but a communal meeting room. The room was large compared to my cell, but nowhere near the size of the laundry room. The grey walls were covered with paper ranging from pocket-sized scraps to massive sheets larger than me. At a glance I recognized some of the scrawl as notes. There were Tribe names, weapons lists, and maps covering the pages. Before I could take a closer look, a woman cleared her throat.

Arstid rose from a high back chair hidden in the shadows of a rather large bookcase. There was a tattered book clutched in her bony hand. As she moved towards us, her body slipped into its customary military stance. Nothing about this woman ever seemed at ease, her face pinched, her body always rigid as if ready for an attack. I wondered if anyone had ever offered to remove the pole from her rear end.

I tried to relax my stance, to not look like her. But based on the quizzical look Triven shot me, I had only managed to look awkward.

"Triven you are dismissed, I can handle her from here."

She nodded curtly at him, but he didn't move.

"If it is permissible, I would prefer to remain here."

"Fine." Arstid said curtly, obviously irritated. "Just sit in the corner and keep your thoughts to yourself."

I stared at him in disbelief. Who was this man that he could stay Maddox and speak out against their leader's wishes? Without another glance in my direction, Triven settled himself into a chair and folded his hands waiting for her to continue.

Arstid pinched the bridge of her nose while gesturing with her other hand. "Please take a seat Phoenix."

I chose a stiff chair. "Will you be providing me with some of the answers you so righteously promised, or are we going to continue with another round of pointless questions?"

Her returning glare pleased me. "Actually Phoenix, yes I will be providing you with answers as I see fit. And you in return are going to answer some of mine."

I raised my eyebrows waiting for her questions, but instead she surprised me, providing answers to questions I had long been asking.

"As you have surely noticed during your confinement here, we do not follow the rules of Tartarus, nor will we tolerate those who do. Within our walls, all captives will be treated as a threat unless proven otherwise. And those who cannot be trusted will be terminated."

Triven shifted behind me.

"For six years we have gathered allies and in return gained information about the Tribes. Our community is comprised of excommunicated Tribesman and those of us who were foolish enough to follow your mother from The Sanctuary. We call ourselves The Subversive."

My eyes widened. "That makes six Tribes…"

Arstid's white head shook slowly. "No. We are *not* a Tribe. The Subversive was created in *spite* of the Tribes. Unlike the uncouth clans that formed within this vile city to rule and murder, we joined together out of necessity. Alone we were weak and vulnerable, together we are strong and knowledgeable."

My eyes narrowed. This was a recruitment speech.

"The fact that you managed to survive in this city alone as long as you have speaks great lengths about your intellect. Unless you have merely been very *lucky*."

Her words stung.

"I don't believe in luck." I said through my teeth.

"Funny, neither do I." Her bright eyes were like stones. "That is why I am hesitantly offering this deal. You will get no time to think or sleep on it. The second you walk out this door the deal is off the table.

"Three days a week you will work wherever we sit fit, earning your keep within this society. The other four you will be operating either with myself or another member of the guard. You will answer all questions we ask you and you *will* be forthright. In return I will provide you with the information we have gathered both about the Tribes and The Sanctuary."

"And what if I don't have the information you want?" I held her gaze.

"Your father's notebook has obviously proven key to your survival here. To your advantage, most of his notes are coded and unreadable. I guarantee that between what's in that pretty little head of yours and what's scrawled in the journal, we can find a compromise."

"And what will you do with that information?" I asked bluntly.

"Whatever we want to. If you prove useful, you may be privy to our plans. But until that point you will do as you're told and play nice. If you cannot adhere to these guidelines the ramifications will be permanent." Her chest rose and fell evenly as she awaited my answer.

Unfortunately, it didn't feel like I was being given much of a choice. I seriously contemplated bashing in her smug face with my chair and rejoicing until the guards came for me, but a noise distracted me. Triven cleared his throat and I was reminded of those who needed me here. Of Mouse, who I promised I would return to.

"We have a deal." My jaw clenched as the words slipped out.

To my surprise Arstid's face did not break out into the smug smile I had expected. Instead her gaze hardened, as if she had wanted me to lash out, to defy her.

"We have a deal."

Arden and Mouse were both waiting for me when I returned to our cell, their anxiety clearly dissipating when they saw me. We ate in silence until the lights turned out, my eyes constantly gravitating to the vent behind Arden's bed. As Mouse's breaths turned to light snores, Arden finally spoke to me.

"Do you think you'll run if you get the chance?" His voice was barely a whisper.

"I'm afraid that chance has already passed." I said and rolled over.

7. RESISTANCE

The tattered paper of my father's notebook crinkled beneath my fingers. I traced his writing with a heavy heart. I hated that I was giving away my father's last words, the words that had kept me safe for so many years. I had already shared too much, given the last part of my parents I had to a stranger. A stranger I didn't even trust.

Arstid's pen tapped on the table, her impatience obvious. I ground my teeth thinking of Mouse again. I was doing this to protect the child, I reminded myself, to keep her from growing up alone and angry like I had. I took a deep breath before continuing.

"He wrote about what objects were good to trade. The basic necessities everyone needs to survive like food, water, shelter and clothing. This page is about seeking out other rogues in the city, possible locations they might hide." I stopped, closing my father's notebook. "That's it essentially. I don't know what else you thought you would find in his notes."

Arstid sat back pressing the pen to her mouth. "I have to admit it's not exactly what we had hoped for. The majority is just about survival skills. I had hoped there would be more about The Sanctuary or... I don't know... *something* more."

Disappointment etched her pointed face.

"Well I held up my end of the deal." I said, reminding her I had played by the rules.

She waved me off. "I can't believe you survived as long as you did on your own. I assumed your father's book held something we didn't know, but apparently you *were* just lucky." She spit the word at me, knowing my distaste for it.

My jaw tightened. "Yeah, lucky."

Because watching your parents get murdered was lucky. Growing up filled with hatred and distrust was lucky. I survived because I chose to, because I learned to take care of myself, because of my parents' words. To her they were nothing, but to me they were the difference between life and death. And it was my choice, not luck, to withhold things that I knew, things that I didn't write in the book. Fortunately, the book's tattered state had hidden the page I ripped out. It was the only page I had ever removed from the book. It was also the best advice my father gave me.

"Don't write everything down. Your thoughts and your knowledge are your own. If it is written down it can be stolen. The safest place in the world is in your own mind, no one can ever steal that from you."

He was right. If being callous had taught me anything, it was how to keep a straight face while lying. Whenever Arstid's keen eyes scrutinized me, I gave nothing away.

She knew how I moved from safe house to safe house at random. That I stole most of my reserves from the Ravagers—my own private attempt to weaken them one worthless bag of dried food at a time. She even knew about the Healer, but there were things I kept from her. Like the locations of more than half of my safe houses, every other outcast I traded with and what my real name was. Arstid knew my mother, but only by her first name. Apparently, The Sanctuary's rebellion didn't deal so well in trust either. She had told me very little about my parents except the fact that they were all from The Sanctuary, and that was about to change. It had been a week since we started our little meetings, and she owed me answers.

Crossing my arms, I fixed the white-haired woman in my gaze. "Your turn."

Her snowy eyebrows rose, "Already bored of our little arrangement?"

"I have upheld my end of the deal and you have yet to uphold yours. I don't believe you're a deceitful person. Are you Arstid?" I smiled sweetly.

Her eyes narrowed.

"No, I am not. But the information I choose to share with you is privileged and if you divulge it to anyone outside of our walls, your death will not be gentle."

"I wouldn't expect anything less." I wasn't scared of this woman. "What exactly *is* your objective here? You once lived within The Wall and yet you chose to leave. That could not have been without reason."

"How much do you remember of your time within The Wall, Phoenix?"

It bothered me that she had not answered my question.

"Not very much." This was an honest answer. "I remember reading with my father, my mother pushing me on a swing and my father carrying me through a tunnel to get here. Just small flashes of a meaningless childhood."

"I know the tunnel you speak of. It is the same one that my family came through. As did the other members of the resistance. In all of your searches have you ever found it again?"

"No." I had looked too. It was as if the city swallowed it whole.

"As the last of our members were coming through, the Minister had it blown up. Thirty-five people were buried alive in the blast. Only eleven of us managed to escape the city, and of those eleven, there are now only five of us left. Yourself included."

The room fell silent as she waited for my response. When I said nothing, she continued.

"Your parents were the first through, as they were our leaders at the time. You can imagine how it looked when they were the only ones who managed to escape the tunnels unscathed. Someone had tipped off the Minister about our escape and then, when your parents were the only ones who didn't make it to the rendezvous point it wasn't hard to put the pieces together. We found their bodies not long after and assumed justice had been served. Now, in hindsight, it appears we may have been a little hasty in our judgments. But you can't blame me for trusting my instincts." She cast me a pointed look, implying she still did not trust my parents. And that she also felt the apple didn't fall far from the tree. "It was presumed you died with them. Apparently, we were mistaken."

"Apparently." I agreed with a bitter smile, trying to swallow back the hatred I felt for her. How dare she imply my mother's betrayal.

The noise of someone stirring behind me reminded me we were not alone. While I would never admit it, I was pleased that Triven had become my new guard.

Arstid continued, ignoring him. "All of our leaders were dead— either killed in the blast or murdered by the Tribes. Your mother, being one of them. Those of us who were left became stranded in this hellhole. If it weren't for our knowledge of this barracks we would all be dead."

"Barracks?" I looked closer at the cement walls surrounding us.

"This was an old military bunker, designed to save lives when The Devastation came. Once the world came to a standstill, its inhabitants left and sought out a new society. Soon thereafter, The Sanctuary was built and the Tribes were born. Fortunately for us, this place was forgotten."

"So we're underground?" My stomach rolled.

"Actually, we are pressed into the mountains that encase our fair city."

It wasn't the sewers, but it still felt harder to breath.

"You obviously hate this place as much as I do. Why

70

did you leave The Sanctuary to come here?" I wondered.

"I suppose it is the Grass is Greener Theory. Tartarus may be a horrific place, but at least the Tribes embrace it. They don't try to paint it as something it's not. Inside The Wall, the government covers up their terribleness. Instead of being forthright, the government disguises their horrific actions with things like laws and self-proclaimed morality. At least here, you *know* you can't trust anyone." She looked pointedly at me. "While your mother may not have been the one who betrayed us, she was the one who led us here. And I would be lying if I said I wasn't harboring a grudge. If we knew what it would cost us, no one would have come. I loathe both The Sanctuary and Tartarus. One city threatened to destroy my family and the other did. This city tore my life apart. It took my husband from me. And now both cities must pay."

Arstid was right. You couldn't trust anyone here, but the fastest way to unite people was to give them a common enemy. Regardless of what she thought about my parents and despite our distaste for one another, we sought the same goal, to see someone suffer for the loss of our families. These cities had robbed us of the only things we cared about and someone deserved to pay.

"It is our goal to infiltrate The Wall and bring down The Sanctuary from within, but to do that we must first overpower the Tribes. Justice is not something this world has seen in hundreds of years, and it is time someone started administering it."

If destroying hell meant partnering with the devil, it was a risk I was willing to take.

"I'm in."

8. JUDGMENT

The unfortunate part of caring about a person other than yourself, is that you become tethered to that someone. Suddenly every action you make has double the consequences, which not only affect yourself, but that other person as well.

I hated that feeling.

I have never had to think about anyone else before. Since the day my parents died, I have only had to think about my own survival. But now there were two of us to think about. I couldn't even say what made me feel so protective of Mouse. Maybe it was that she reminded me of myself, a small child alone in the world. Not the me now, but the little girl who died that day in the alley with her parents. *That* little girl.

Maybe it was the way she exuded innocence, the way a child should. Maybe it was the way she looked at people with trusting eyes. The way she turned to me for protection, even though I was not the most trustworthy person. Still she looked to me for security, clung to my side when she was frightened. Mouse looked at me like I was a better person, and for her sake I wanted to be.

I just wasn't sure I could be.

Some things that are broken stay broken. There is no

putting the pieces back together.

The dreams still haunted me every morning. Nothing could change that. Even with the tiny, fragile body sleeping beneath my cot, a fresh scream caught in my throat choking me awake every day. Those dreams reminded me why I didn't want to get close to others. Why I had chosen to be a recluse. After starting awake I would stare at the vent hidden behind Arden's bed. Plans would form and my legs would itch for freedom.

Then the tiny hand would creep over the edge of my bed and I would stay.

We had found an odd rhythm to our days in captivity. A small part of me felt comfort in the routine. Every day was new, but the expectancies were the same— eat, work, divulge my secrets, eat, work, sleep. Each day moved like the consistent tick of my father's pocket watch. That's why when I awoke this morning I knew something was different.

When I jolted from my bed I could feel the room was different, that something was off. Even in the dark, I could feel it. Searching the barren room, my eyes lit on Arden's bed.

It was empty.

I had heard him come in after lights out. I was sure of it.

Wasn't I?

After working long days with Triven, I had begun to sleep too hard. I didn't hear as much as I should have. A month ago I would have heard a moth's wings and now I couldn't remember whether or not a man had walked just three feet from me.

Matters only got worse when the lights came on. His bed was made. No, he did not sleep here last night.

As the footsteps came down the hall, the accusing words were out of my mouth before Triven could walk in.

"What have you done with Arden?"

No, not Triven.

Every nerve stood at attention as Maddox's black eyes leered at me. I moved between him and Mouse, shielding her

73

from his view.

"What, not happy to see your old friend?" Maddox taunted.

"Where is Arden?" I asked again.

"You'll find out soon enough."

Moving with surprising speed he grabbed my upper arm and yanked me against his chest, lifting me painfully, until my face was inches from his.

"Reckoning time has come." His breath smelled foul.

I wanted to punch him. Break his nose and laugh as the blood poured down his chin. But Mouse was watching, her tiny feet shuffling behind us. I swallowed to keep from spitting in his smug face.

Someone else was coming, his or her footsteps rapidly approaching. Maddox kept his grip, but pushed me further away. I found myself actually hoping for Triven's face to appear in the doorway, but I was disappointed. Veyron's blonde head came into view as she pressed her hand to the scanner. Her blue eyes narrowed at us, but she said nothing.

"Mouse, do you want to go get some breakfast with me before class?" Veyron's tone was motherly and comforting but Mouse recoiled from her. Her stringy hair draped her worried face as she shook her head. Normally she would have clung to my side, but it was obvious she was scared of Maddox.

"Mouse, you should go with Veyron. I am sure there is a wonderful breakfast waiting for you." I was trying to keep my voice even, but she shook her head again.

I knew this day would come, the day they would tire of me. Since I arrived I knew it was only a matter of time before they disposed of me. She on the other hand was only a child. If I could keep her away from me she could still survive.

"Mouse, you have to go with her." Her tears began to well, so I did the only thing I could. I lied. "Don't cry silly. I just want to make sure you save me a seat. Maddox here is taking me to meet with Triven for a minute, but we are all going to be starving when we get back. So you had better save

74

us some good stuff, okay?"

Her doe eyes were hesitant.

"Right Maddox?" I said through gritted teeth glaring at him.

"Right. Don't worry Mouse, this won't take long." His smile was a little too harsh to be genuine.

I rearranged my expression before turning back to her. I think I smiled.

I watched as she took Veyron's hand and followed her out of the cell. Her brown eyes were wide as she disappeared around the corner. I couldn't speak. I knew I should have said something to soothe her further, found words to encourage her. But my mother's last words had haunted me and I didn't want to haunt Mouse.

I didn't get the chance to mourn losing my small friend and truthfully it was better that way. As soon as their footfalls faded away, Maddox grabbed my bag with my few possessions safe inside and dragged me from the cell. I thought idly of the vent, but it was too late now. I didn't fight as he dragged me through the tunnels. It was pointless. Even if I managed to overpower him, there was nowhere to go. Plus I was tired. The world had beaten me down over and over again. Before I was just too stupid to stay down. Not this time.

At first I feared Maddox might be the one to do it, but he moved with too much quickened ferocity. If he was taking me for his own pleasure, he would have taken his time, enjoyed my discomfort. No, he was not enjoying this. He was moving on someone else's orders. This was business not pleasure. Still, his fingers dug into my arm and I knew they would leave marks. At least I wouldn't see my end at his hands. I wanted to stay down this time and let the world finally win. But if it were at his hands I would not go quietly. In fact, I was pretty sure I would kill him first if given the chance.

The curved walls all looked the same, but I knew them now. Even in the despairing sea of grey concrete, I knew we were going to the meeting room crammed with furniture. The rapture had come and no one can outrun their offenses forever.

His fingers didn't loosen when he knocked on the doors. I am not sure what I expected when the doors finally opened, but it definitely wasn't what I saw. The room was filled with people. Some of them I recognized, but the most predominate face in the crowd was Triven's. His hazel eyes tightened as they fell on Maddox's grip on my arm. The room was buzzing like angry bees.

"Quiet down please." I hadn't even noticed Arstid until she spoke. She was sitting at the round table looking intently at me. "We have been called here today to pass judgment on this young woman."

My face tightened. I wasn't just being sentenced. I was being put on trial.

"This young specimen was found in an alley trying to protect the mute child from the Ravagers. Single-handedly, she was able to kill three Tribe members and permanently blind one."

That was a fact I was proud of, but the tone in Arstid's voice was far too contemptuous for my liking. I had a bad feeling where she was going with this.

"Since arriving here, she has proven frequently uncooperative, mistrusting and prone to outbursts of violence. She has run as a lone wolf for the majority of her young life and while intelligent, also proves obstinate."

I could show her a real outburst right now.

"That being said, she has divulged how she managed to remain alive in Tartarus for so long. While not all of the information is pertinent to us, she is also the only person to enter our population who has infiltrated the Ravagers' safe houses."

Several heads turned to me in surprise. The others looked at me with doubt.

"I know where I stand on her sentencing, but this is an egalitarianism judgment not a Tribe ruling. We will hear from her handler, then judgment will be passed by majority vote."

I tore my eyes away from hers, turning to face the other twenty people in turn. If they were going to put me down, then they would have to remember me. I suppressed a gasp of shock as two familiar deep brown eyes met mine. Arden stood beside the blonde guard I met the first day. He looked... ashamed. To my surprise it was he who stepped forward to speak and not Triven as I had expected.

His Adam's apple bobbed wildly as he searched for the words. He wouldn't meet my eyes. "I... I was placed in Phoenix's cell to assess her. While distrusting at times, I never found her to be violent or overly deceitful. Like all of us, she obviously has her secrets, but that did not impede her ability to communicate in a friendly manner with me. Once the child was released into her care, Phoenix became more cautious with her actions, always putting the child's safety above her own desires. Despite being a recluse for so long, humanity is still ingrained in her."

I flushed with anger. I knew he was trying to help me, to make me look like the good guy, but he was also making me look weak. And he had lied—I had never been friendly. I bit the inside of my cheek to keep from screaming at his traitorous face.

"Upon revealing the vent to her, which could have been an easy escape, Phoenix still chose to stay. She said the time for escaping had passed. I don't think she is a flight risk and I believe she could prove a strong attribute to our community."

Finally his eyes met mine. His brown stare was repentant and admiring all at once. I was sure my returning gaze was not as friendly. What did he mean "attribute to their community?"

Murmurs began to swirl around the room again.

With a flicker of her hand Arstid silenced them.

"Those for termination." A heart-dropping number of hands rose, Arstid's being one of the first.

"Those for integration." Her pinched face looked smug as if she already knew the answer.

Maddox's hand tightened, undoubtedly hungry to throw me to the wolves. I looked at the worn tabletop. I didn't need to see death coming for me.

The sound of skin moving against fabric, of the low steady breathing was deafening. Why didn't she just say it already?

Termination.

Say it. *Termination.*

"Integration."

I was sure I had heard her wrong. My eyes darted toward her face. She looked as if she had just smelled something foul.

"According to law, someone must take responsibility for her." Her thin lips had nearly disappeared.

"I will." The response was immediate. All heads turned to see who had spoken, but I knew that voice. What surprised me was that Arden's mouth had opened to speak too, but Triven was faster. Maddox's fingers were beyond excruciating on my arm as Dr. Porters fidgeted in the back, hidden next to a bookcase.

Arstid looked furious, her usually pallid face flushed. She spoke through her teeth, "Fine. Triven, she is yours to watch. Meeting adjourned."

The bodies filtered out of the room quickly now. It was easy to pick out those who had wished for my termination. Their quickly moving feet skirted me with a wide berth, their eyes averted from the girl they had just condemned. Triven appeared out of the crowd, his steady gaze fixed on my arm still in Maddox's grip.

"Maddox." He said raising his eyes.

The behemoth did not release me, but his grip loosened. Taking full advantage, I ripped my arm from his hold. I was pleased when his balance faltered as I yanked away. Maybe he wasn't as strong as I had thought he was. Big man could be shaken by a little girl. The air was practically vibrating between the two men. Someone else must have sensed the tension, because a heavy hand fell on Maddox's shoulder. It was the blonde guard with the ponytail.

"Come on man. Let's get something to eat."

Shoving his friend's hand from his shoulder he pushed his way through the room. The blonde guard shrugged at us and followed.

We waited until the room had emptied, until our quiet breathing was the only sound that could be heard. Even the echoing footsteps had fallen away. Triven stood behind me and I kept my back to him. For some reason it didn't bother me like it should have anymore.

"Now what?" I asked looking at the open doors.

"Now you get the tour." He walked past me without glancing to see if I followed.

Despite myself, I did follow. Grabbing my bag Maddox had unceremoniously dumped on the floor, I jogged out the doors after Triven.

It was strange moving through the tunneled halls now. No guard pointing a weapon at me or wrenching my arm from its socket. Triven acted as he always did, nonchalant and careful not to touch me. But it still felt different. Now that I thought about it, unlike any of the other guards, he never touched me. With him I was allowed a personal bubble.

But I was no fool. Even though I moved through these halls no longer a prisoner, I was still far from free.

9. LEASHED

I had followed Triven's broad shoulders through doors I had never seen before, through rooms that spanned from the size of my cell to the huge size of the laundry room. Everything looked the same. Grey walls, grey floors, no windows. Everything *was* the same. I supposed that should be expected of an old bunker. What I didn't anticipate was the number of rooms and how self-sustaining the compound was. There were water filtration rooms that generated power while cleaning the water, and grow rooms filled with soils and artificial lights. Strange vegetation grew in those rooms, some I recognized like the apple trees, but others were foreign to me.

People lingered, watching us with curious eyes. Some even turned, whispering to each other as they eyed me. Apparently I already had a reputation here and from the nervous twitch of their lips it wasn't a good one. I shouldn't have, but I smiled at them. Not in the friendly, "we should chat sometime" kind of way. But in the "yeah those stories are true, you might not want to get too close to me" kind of way.

My mother never said make friends, she said survive. And in my experience that did not include making friends.

The mess hall was empty by the time we reached it and

I worried about Mouse. Now that my impending death had been put on hold, I felt horrible for lying to her. I was sure those tiny hands would be ringing over one another, anxious and alone. Once our tour was complete I would have to find her. It wasn't the same with her. I wasn't looking for a friend or a little sister, but while I sought no comfort in her, I sought to comfort her. I needed no one, but Mouse? She needed someone. She needed me.

As we marched through what felt like the hundredth tunnel that looked like every other tunnel, I began to lose my patience.

"So what is this then, some weird colony thing? Are we like married now or something?" I asked Triven's back.

He scoffed. "This is a trial to see if you would be a good fit for us and us for you."

"And when it doesn't work out?"

He shrugged, "*If* that happens you will be free to go. I will see to that myself. But maybe you should give us a chance before writing us off. You may actually like it here."

It was my turn to scoff. "I highly doubt that."

Shrugging off my negativity, he smiled. "You might be surprised."

He had paused outside a metal door with faded blue paint peeling off. Pushing the door open, he gestured for me to enter first. As I entered the dark room, my fingers fluttered automatically to where my holster used to be, finding only linen fabric instead of cool metal.

Old habits die hard.

It was darker in the small room than it had been in the hallway. A lonely bulb hung from the ceiling without a shade, its black cord disappearing into the darkness above without revealing a ceiling. I could see the floor, the outline of what looked like a bed and dark looming walls that were covered in some sort of lumpy texture, like mismatched bricks.

"Watch your eyes." Triven warned.

I heard a switch flip and the bulb intensified, throwing

the room into brightness. I gasped. I couldn't help it.

The walls were not bricks. They were books, hundreds and hundreds of books.

The worn covers lined every curved wall. Some stacks came to my knees while others scaled high above my head. A neat pile was stacked next to the bed, the top one open, face down to hold a page. I touched the leather bindings closest to me.

Without thinking I leaned in and took a deep breath. The perfumed scent of aged paper and ink swirled around me. I closed my eyes, reveling in the smell that made me think of my father. Tracing my fingers over the rows, I scanned the titles. There were books I had read, ones I had never heard of and authors whose names I recognized. I would have thought this was their library except for the bed in the corner.

I turned to Triven. He was leaning on the doorframe watching me, his hazel eyes bright.

It clicked.

"You're the one who read to me in the infirmary."

He actually blushed.

"I didn't think you would remember that." Triven toed the concrete.

Shifting awkwardly I changed the subject.

"So is this your room?" I went back to reading titles.

"Technically it's *our* room now."

I whipped back to him, my neck cricking a little with the speed.

"*Excuse* me?"

"Normally a trial candidate is paired with someone of the same sex, but in your case I figured you would be most comfortable with me."

I raised my eyebrows at him.

"I have seen how you are with other people and to be honest I think quite a few of them are afraid of you. But with me you don't seem quite as... tense."

I stared hard at him looking for any sign of ruse. My

gaze shifted to the only bed in the corner of the room. His eyes followed.

"You and Mouse can have the bed. Arden is bringing me a cot. Don't worry, we won't have to share."

I continued to stare blankly at him.

"I know it's not ideal..." He looked hurt.

Somehow I had offended him. I suppressed the urge to roll my eyes. A month ago I wouldn't have cared, but today guilt seeped into my emotions.

"Mouse won't sleep on the bed, so I will take the cot. There is no point putting you out any more than I already have." I didn't want to owe him anything. He had already volunteered to be my sponsor. I didn't need to add taking his bed to that list.

He opened his mouth to protest but seemed to think better of it, simply shrugging. I had a feeling this wouldn't be the last of the conversation.

Throwing my bag next to his bed, I sat and picked up the splayed book. It was a novel by Charles Dickens. I repressed a smile as I turned to him.

"I'm surprised you can read, not many can anymore."

"I could say the same about you."

I thought he was teasing me.

"My mother taught me to read. She thought it was important that our generations' educations not be lost. I now teach other defectors to read as well." He picked up a random book from the pile, running his fingers over the title. "I guess you could call this The Subversive library."

I smiled at him. I am not sure what came over me but I actually smiled at him. His returning grin was equally surprising. Not wanting this strange moment of comradery to go too far, I began to press for more answers.

"So, my being here was a setup from the beginning. Your people have been testing me since the moment I arrived."

That wiped the smile from his face.

"Yes." He put the book back, the moment gone. "You

know better than anyone else how hard it is to trust someone in Tartarus. We must take every precaution possible before exposing you to our people."

"You still don't trust me though."

He sighed, folding his arms. "You're different than anyone else we have come across. The people we rescue from the streets always come from a Tribe. Everyone defects for his or her own reason, but ultimately they *chose* to leave. You on the other hand were a loner. You weren't disengaging from allegiances to free yourself, you were already free. Your only alliance was to yourself."

I stared hard at a crack in the floor. "No one is free in Tartarus."

He was quiet for a moment. "I agree, but unfortunately not everyone sees it that way. They see you as an anomaly to the system, and people fear what they don't understand."

He was right. If I wasn't one of them, then I was against them. Even if this wasn't a Tribe, the "Join or Die" mentality still lived in their every breath. I suddenly felt like a rodent trapped in a very large cage of hungry cats.

"How would you feel about letting off a little steam?" Triven was watching my left leg that had begun to bounce rapidly.

My body went rigid as he stepped toward me, his hand raising. He stepped back immediately. Without saying another word he turned and walked out the door. I sat for about two heartbeats before going after him. I caught up just as he turned the corner.

"Don't we have work we should be doing or another pointless meeting with Arstid?" I actually felt bad for my reaction to his friendly overtures.

"Today is my free day and since you are now in my care, it is also your free day."

"Shouldn't we go find Mouse then?" I said, the little girl still on my mind.

"We will meet her for dinner, but in the meantime I

figure it might be nice to stretch your legs." He pushed aside two large doors as we entered a cavernous room that had not been on the tour.

The walls were lined with weaponry from training batons to hand guns, even tiny silver throwing knives hung neatly in a row next to a larger blade resembling a machete. Huge bags, larger than me, hung from the arched ceiling and stalls lined the far end of the room, forming some kind of shooting range. In the center of the room was an elevated black mat, where two men now stood watching us. In fact, everyone in the room had stopped what they were doing and were now staring at us.

"This is our training room." Triven ignored the stares and continued to speak. "All residents are encouraged to train here once they are of age. Weapons must stay in this room at all times. Removing one will have dire consequences."

A darker skinned girl at the firing range twitched the gun in her right hand as if she would have liked to use me for practice.

Or maybe it was just a nervous spasm.

As if reading my mind, her eyes narrowed. Raising the hand with the gun she fired at the target making five clean tightly placed shots.

Not nerves then.

After a moment, I noticed why she had fired with only one hand. Dangling where her left hand should have been was a gnarled stump. Apparently Doc Porter's cell regeneration stuff could heal but not re-grow lost limbs. She must have been a Wraith or at least crossed one. Too bad for them she appeared to be a righty.

She laid down her gun and approached us with long strides. She might have been my age, maybe a little older, but she had almost a foot on me. Her long slender body was nothing but muscle. Her eyes were a rich brown. To any man she would have been attractive but to me she looked like a threat. Her expression was far from friendly.

85

"Do you really think this is a good idea?" She was nearly as tall as Triven and more intimidating.

Triven merely shrugged. "Does it really matter? It's my head not yours if she screws up."

"You'd be wise to remember that." Her chocolate eyes shifted to mine, sizing me up. "Hurt him and I will kill you myself."

"Duly noted."

She slammed into my shoulder as she pushed past us. It took all of my control not to jump on her back as she walked out. Several others followed closely behind her.

"Girlfriend of yours?" I glared after the tall girl.

"Archer? No, she's just a good friend."

"Nice friends." I mumbled.

"Coming from the girl who has so many." He laughed.

That brought me up short.

"So, what sounds good?" He raised his hands offering me the entire training room.

Was this another test? What better way to assess my skills than make it seem like basic training.

And I *was* skilled.

I had not survived Tartarus without training. Training I had traded a good deal for. But no one needed to know the full extent of my capabilities, not even my tender book-reading guardian.

"Knives?" I needed to prove I wasn't afraid to touch the weapons here *and* that I wouldn't turn on him. Besides, if he witnessed the incident in the alley when I saved Mouse, he probably already knew my skills with a knife.

Triven gestured for me to lead the way. Choosing the throwing knives, I collected six, offering him three.

"Ladies first." He pointed to the target at the end of the room. It was nothing more than a block of wood with chunks carved out of it from repetitive target practice.

Cringing internally at his remark, I stepped in line with my target. I flipped the blade in my hand, feeling its weight, testing its balance. It was larger than the knives I usually carried. The hilt was heavy and unfamiliar in my hand.

Triven cleared his throat.

Resisting the urge to glare at him, I drew back and at a calculated interval snapped my arm forward at the elbow releasing the knife. The hollow thunk as it penetrated the wood was satisfying, but my aim was rusty. The handle quivered as the blade stuck in the left top corner. I had been aiming for the center.

Triven mirrored my stance and let his knife fly. It connected with the center of the board.

To my frustration he was suppressing a smile.

If this was a game, I was losing.

My next throw was more on mark, landing less than an inch from his. His next throw fell wide, barely hitting the post.

My turn to smile. Maybe that first throw was just lucky.

We didn't speak as we practiced. Each time we finished a round Triven would collect the knives and we would start our silent challenge again. After realizing I wasn't going to go on a killing spree, people began to continue with their own training.

It was eye-opening.

Every time Triven left to retrieve our weapons I watched them.

There were men and women alike, and to my surprise they were all skilled. I was particularly interested in the two men sparring. Hand-to-hand combat was something that had been nearly lost in the past century. An ancient art traded in for modern weapons. But both of these men moved with sinuous control. Their bodies were the only weapons they needed. When your body is your weapon, you don't need to rely on guns for protection.

That's the funny thing about guns; even untrained hands can feel powerful using them. But take that gun away and you're left with nothing but a coward whose only skill is how to blindly pull a trigger.

But men like these— men trained to defend

themselves, to defend others— take the gun from their hands and they could still kill you.

I knew how to move like they were and I had paid handsomely to do so.

Triven placed a knife in my hand. "Care to make this interesting?"

My eyebrows rose, "What did you have in mind?"

"Whoever gets closest to the center of the X gets the cot. Loser takes the bed." He thrust his open hand to me offering a deal.

I glanced at the X he had carved into the post. This would be easy.

I took his deal, putting my hand in his. It was the first time we had ever touched. I was surprised how warm his rough hands were, how easily they fit over mine. I snatched my hand back, wiping my palm reflexively against my thigh.

I turned to the post, not to be out-done.

"Ladies first," I reminded him. A smug smile crept to my lips. The tip of my blade was imbedded in the whittled surface less than an eighth of an inch from the center of the X.

I win.

I turned to Triven, my smile still lingering.

"Nice throw." He nodded, impressed, turning his hazel eyes on me. "But you could work on your stance a bit."

Without breaking eye contact, he whipped his arm forward. My eyes naturally followed the knife as it left his hand and the smile fell from my face. A small spark emitted as the tip of his blade grazed mine and rooted itself dead center of the X.

"I guess I will be taking the cot tonight." He said, with a smile.

10. NIGHTMARES

My underestimation of Triven bothered me. My ability to assess people had kept me alive on the streets but with him I had been wrong. For six years, I could pick out a threat from a mile away. But Triven had gotten close. I had let him get close. And for some unknown reason, no buzzer in my brain went off. There was no warning of an imposing threat. Yet, clearly he was not just a sensitive bookworm.

His knife-throwing abilities had proven that. I waited for my intuition to whisper its warning, but still there was only silence.

A part of me hoped it was because he wasn't a threat, and the other part of me told the first part to shut up, that I was growing soft.

We found Mouse at dinnertime. She was sitting with several other small children, pushing her food around her plate. It wasn't until she saw me that her face lit up. Her quick smile warmed something in my heart. Launching herself from the table, Mouse ran to us. The impact as she crashed into me was surprising for how small she was. There were tears spilling down her cheeks as her frail arms wrapped around me.

"Hey," I crouched and wiped them away with my

sleeve. "I promised I would come back didn't I?"

She nodded, her chin still quivering.

"I won't let anything happen to you, okay?" There was no promise of staying here with her this time. I didn't want to lie again. Not to her.

"How about you and I go get some dinner while Phoenix finds us a seat." Triven offered Mouse his hand.

To my surprise she took it, letting him lead her toward the queuing people waiting for their food. Her doe eyes never stopped watching me, still worried I might bolt if given the chance.

I sighed.

What the hell had I gotten myself into? I was a renegade, a loner. I shouldn't be caring for a child.

As my conscience roiled, I turned to find a table. There were benches and long tables strewn throughout the room. Groups gathered at each, sharing food and talking. Quite a few were staring at me. To my surprise not all gazes were hostile, several possibly even intrigued. But none were welcoming.

There were so many of them. More than I thought. A hundred, maybe more?

A hand waved in the back corner of the room. Arden motioned me to join him and the others at his table. The girl from the training room was there, her dark head turned intentionally away from me.

I wanted to ignore him. To flip him a rude gesture and retreat to Triven's room, but I could feel Mouse's eyes on me. So, instead, I wound through the packed tables to join him. When I sat across from him, something akin to shame tainted his features.

"I'm surprised you came over." He smiled weakly. "I figured you of all people wouldn't have taken my deception very well."

"Perceptive of you." My voice was cold.

"I'm sorry." Arden was actually being sincere. "It's not my favorite job here, but we needed to make sure you could be trusted. There are too many innocent lives here to risk a breach."

His gaze shifted to the table of children and I thawed a little.

"I understand. I would have done the same thing in your shoes." Surprisingly I meant the words as I said them.

Even within the walls of our shared prison, our comradery had been tainted with distrust. He *had* feigned his true identity, but had I not done the same thing? In another time, in another place, we would have been considered children, barely in our teens, but in our world, we both knew better. We weren't children anymore. The cruel world we knew had robbed us of that innocence long ago. And looking at those children sitting at the table laughing as they innocently took comfort in each other, looking at Mouse as she clung to Triven's hand, we both knew we would kill to keep them that way. To give them a chance at what we never had.

I understood Arden's actions. It wasn't even about forgiving him, rather it was about respecting him. And I did. Like me, he was a child of the streets. Raised in a Tribe bent on killing and yet here he had reformed and was now protecting others. Could I follow in those same footsteps or was I too broken? Too far gone?

Guilt tightened my chest as Mouse sat down next to me. Could I be good enough for her?

***

I couldn't sleep that night. The bed was too soft and my thoughts were too loud. Mouse's deep breathing told me she was sleeping soundly beneath me, but Triven was too quiet. His silence gave away his wakefulness, but he said nothing.

"You should have taken the bed." I whispered. A low chuckle responded.

"You shouldn't have underestimated me."

I stared up into the black nothingness above me

listening to him breathe.

"Why am I here, Triven?"

He was silent so long I wondered if he had fallen asleep.

"You have a right to be here just as much as any of us."

That was not the answer I was looking for. "I mean why not let me die in the streets, why save me?"

"Does it really matter why you were saved?" He shifted in his cot.

"To me, it does. Nobody here helps anyone else without expecting something in return."

"But you didn't when you saved Mouse."

My chest tightened. "That's different."

"No it's not. There is still good in people. Sometimes it's hard to see past all of the pain and cruelty, but there are still good people out there. I saw good in you."

I rolled away from him not wanting to talk any more.

"I'm not so sure." I muttered to the wall.

When I awoke it was with my usual stifled scream, my hand pressed hard to my mouth, my legs thrashing in the tangled sheets, my chest heaving with panicked breaths. It took me a minute to realize where I was, and that I was not alone. There was a faint light in the room now. In the murky cast, I could see Triven propped up on his cot with a book in hand and a concerned look on his face.

I pulled my knees to my chest and buried my face. "Sorry."

"Do you wake like that every morning?"

I turned my cold gaze upon him. "Do you ever sleep?"

He still looked sympathetic despite my coolness. "Rarely. The nightmares make it hard to sleep sometimes."

I defrosted a little. Nightmares were a natural part of life in Tartarus. I kept my head pressed to my knees, unable to meet his eyes. Instead, I stared at his hands.

"Yes… I wake up that way every day. Every night I dream of my parents' murders and every morning I choke on the screams of my past. I watch again and again as my parents shove me in a sewer drain to save me. I watch, trapped, as the Ravagers kill my father and rape my mother, before killing her too. I can still smell their blood, hear their screams echoing in my mind. I wake up every day knowing I was too weak to save them."

I never told anyone that. I was not sure why I was telling him now.

"Mine are of my father. He burned to death in a fire started by the Ravagers. We should have all died in it but he saved us. I remember him shielding my body from the flames. The smell of his skin as the fire engulfed him. He threw me from a window to save me. The fall broke my arm but I survived. I watched him burn from the pavement below. His fiery silhouette is still seared on my retinas every time I close my eyes."

When I finally looked up at him, it was his turn to look away. We were both damaged. No one escaped Tartarus unscathed. Mouse stirred beneath me and we both shifted our focus to her. Was she still unscathed? The way she whimpered in her sleep told me she wasn't. Something had happened to her too, but her story was her own. I wasn't sure she would ever be able to share it.

She whimpered again, her tiny hand trembling. I leaned down and squeezed her hand, reassuring her she was safe. She quieted almost instantly.

No. No one escapes Tartarus unscathed.

11. REVERED

The large room felt over-crowded with so many bodies in it. There were not as many gathered as the day of my trial, but there were still too many to feel comfortable. Bodies jostled each other to gain better vantage points around the round table. I was the only one they did not bump into, a wide berth continuously given to me.

I stood behind Triven, who was seated in a chair directly across from Astrid's icy eyes. Her face tightened every time she glanced our way.

It was easy to ascertain that those seated held higher rank. Theirs were the voices that were heard above others, their opinions weighed heavier. I recognized many of these faces as ones I had seen in the training room. The lean, one-armed Archer sat to the left of Astrid, her gaze nearly as cold. Arden was also seated at the table speaking in hushed tones to Veyron. To my disgust, Maddox was also seated at the table, the look in his black eyes hungry as they fell on me. I swallowed back the bile rising in my throat and ignored him.

Arstid's hand raised, signaling for silence. "Where are we on the reconnaissance front?"

Archer was the first to speak. "The city is restless. Tribe

violence is escalating and the Ravagers are at the heart if it. They have managed to get their hands on more weapons and based on the caliber, they are not acquiring them on their own. Someone is helping them. We fear your suspicions were right and that they are working with The Sanctuary."

The room erupted into upheaval at this. There were only three of us who looked unfazed by this news— Triven, Arstid and myself. Her eyes locked on mine as she raised her hand again. Heads swiveled towards me, following her gaze, but she addressed the bald man to her right.

"Have we learned where the exchanges are happening?"

He shook his head. "We have suspicions about their ammunitions warehouse in the lower district. The area is heavily guarded and it seems the most logical place to hide a breach of the wall. We cannot get close on foot, but a team is scheduled to do surveillance from the rooftops at the end of the week. Archer has informed us there is still a building on the fifth block with a scalable drainage pipe—"

"I highly doubt that." The words left my mouth without my full consent.

Archer's glare turned on me. "Are you saying I'm a liar?"

I crossed my arms, returning her stare. "The beige building on the left side of Shaker Street. It's been nearly what? Two months since you investigated that location?"

Her eyes narrowed, confirming my suspicions.

"There is no longer rooftop access there." I smiled at her.

"And how would a pitiless little recluse like you know that?"

"Because I am the one who disabled it." Every eye in the room was now on me.

It was one of the last things I had done before my capture. On a routine check of my accesses I had noticed a scrap of clothing snagged on a loose screw and knew someone had found my access point. I dismantled the pipe that same day.

Recognition sparked in the bald man's eyes. "You're the one who has cut off all roof access throughout the city."

"Not all of it." I shrugged with nonchalance, but knew I had found my golden ticket. No one knew the city's skylines like I did and if they wanted access they were going to need me. The scowl on Arstid's face proved it.

Murmurs began spreading through the room. Everyone was now looking at me with a newfound admiration, even Maddox. The only person stoically unchanged was Triven.

"I always assumed it was a man..."

"I thought it was the Ravagers trying to keep us grounded..."

"She must be lying..."

Apparently I had not been as invisible as I had thought. It seems my legend had preceded me.

Arstid spoke above the rumblings, her face reddening. "If you truly know where the accesses are, you are required to tell us—"

"I am not *required* to tell you anything," I cut her off. There was a collective intake of breath around the room. "But as a sign of good faith I will lead your teams to the access points they seek."

Arstid's taut mouth opened, but it was Triven who spoke first. "I motion to second that proposition."

Several people shouted "Aye" in response. It surprised me that Archer was one of them.

***

After learning of my knowledge, my presence was suddenly desired at every Subversive meeting. Triven and I were constantly relieved of our work duties, were called away from meals and still, I felt we were getting nowhere.

This meeting in particular, seemed to be lasting forever. The balls of my feet had begun to ache and tolerances had begun to wear thin. While half of the room wanted access to The Sanctuary, the other half sought to shut down Tartarus first.

"Take down the leaders and we take down the Tribes." The bald man— whose name I had learned was Willets— spoke as he rubbed his temple in irritation.

I shook my head, for what felt like the thousandth time. "That's the problem with leaders, someone is always waiting to take their place. If we open up that door, the next generation will not be outdone by their predecessors. They're hungrier and their ambitions will prove more dangerous than anything we have witnessed so far."

"She's right. Cutting off its limbs won't kill the city. The Tribes are just pawns, we have to go for the heart. We have to stop The Sanctuary." Arden shouted over the others.

"And we are just supposed to trust your words, that The Sanctuary is actually worse than the Tribes?" Maddox's words rung out over the crowd, "None of us have ever seen what's inside The Wall. How are we to trust you're not lying to us?"

As much as I hated him, his words were valid. Even I couldn't remember much from my days within The Wall, but the few memories I had were better than any I had outside of them.

Willets nodded in agreement. "The Sanctuary is supposed to be a utopia. It is supposed to be a safe place."

I coughed out a sarcastic laugh. "Utopias are not real, human nature sees to that."

Willets' face reddened but several others nodded in agreement.

"But it still has to be better than this," Willets motioned to Archer's missing hand. "It has to be less evil than this."

When Triven finally found his voice for the first time in our meeting, it was barely a whisper. But as he refused to shout, everyone else quieted to hear him. "There is no good or evil here, it all depends on what side you're standing. Nor is it about wrong or right, it's about surviving. And right now we are barely doing that. If we are wrong about The Sanctuary, then is that not the place you want to be? If we are moving toward The Sanctuary— be it to destroy it or join it— at least we are still moving in the right direction for both sides."

There was a murmur of agreement. It amazed me how easily Triven could command the attention of the room. Not only could he command their rapt attention, but they were agreeing with him as well. This boy, maybe a few years older than myself, already showed the signs of being a natural leader. The most curious part was that he had no clue.

Archer spoke, showing her support. "We have never had the numbers, nor the resources to infiltrate The Sanctuary before now. I agree with Triven. Whatever your personal motives are— escaping this city or seeking revenge— our goal is to get into The Sanctuary." She paused before looking at me. "And with our most recent addition, we may actually stand a chance at that goal."

As everyone fell into agreement, the intensity of the meeting passed. People were finalizing plans for our expedition to the Ravagers' warehouse, but I wasn't listening anymore. After Archer spoke, I began to wonder what side I stood on. Did I want to escape back into the city I once called home or did I want revenge for my parents? Was there even revenge for me to seek there?

My forehead creased as I wished I could remember more from my life before their deaths, but there was nothing. Something must have driven my parents to leave, but what? For years I had trusted so blindly that they had left for a good reason, but as I grew older that was becoming harder and harder to believe. I had seen too many horrible things here to imagine worse. When I was ten, I never questioned my parents' reasons or wondered what kind of people they were. To me, they were perfect—but look at the way Mouse looked at me now. Her innocent eyes saw nothing of the terrible, hardened person I knew I was inside. Her jaded perception, now made me question my own.

What if my parents weren't the saints I had made them out to be? What if Arstid's accusations were true and they had led all those people to slaughter?

I cursed myself for thinking it.

So was I escaping or avenging? Honestly, I wasn't sure. Maybe I just wanted to see it all burn.

12. UNBOUND

I had become less of a peculiarity around The Subversive now. I walked the halls alone, unguarded, and no one stopped me. Oddly enough, some people even nodded or smiled as I passed. I was not entirely sure when it happened, but gradually people stared at me less, their wary eyes growing bored.

Well, most of them.

Arstid still watched me like a hawk. Her penetrating eyes constantly flickered from mine to Mouse, reminding me that my actions no longer affected only myself. As if to say, "Screw up and she will pay the price."

Arstid had me on a short leash and she knew it.

Triven and I had fallen into a rhythm. We worked side by side every day, trained most nights together and met with the guard when called for. I had even become accustomed to sharing a room with him and had begun to find his ever-wakeful presence reassuring. When I awoke like a frightened child every morning, the light from his reading lamp soothed me. His warm eyes would meet mine and he would hand me something to read, something to distract my mind from the nightmares.

We never talked about it again after that first night.

Mouse was making friends and while she still slept beneath my bed, her whimpering had dissipated. While I was still unsure of what *I* was doing here, I could see a future for her.

Tonight, Triven's light snores let me know he was actually sleeping for a change. It was a steady reminder of what I should be doing as well, but my mind refused to turn off.

We were leaving tomorrow night for the reconnaissance mission of the Ravagers' weapons warehouse and my mind refused to forget that. I knew that I needed the rest, that I must be on point, but the voices in my head wouldn't stop nagging. This would be the first time I had been outside the bunker since my capture. And it could be the only opportunity I got, the only chance I would have to run.

But did I want to run?

My head throbbed. Less than a month ago I wanted nothing more than to be free of these people and now… What? I wanted to stay?

No.

But I didn't really want to leave either. When did this get so complicated?

Careful not to wake Mouse or Triven, I slipped into the hall. I needed time away from them. Away from their familiar breathing and comforting sounds.

My feet carried me to the training room before I realized that's where I wanted to go. The halls were empty. I passed not a soul along the way.

When I entered the room it was dimly lit. Only half of the lights were on to conserve energy. A pool of light focused on the sparring mat. It should have frightened me— it would have frightened a normal person— but to me the darkness was inviting. A place to hide.

Removing my tattered long-sleeved shirt, I entered the ring and began to stretch. It was freeing that there were no cameras here, no way to keep tabs on me. I wasn't sure the limited power running in the barracks could even support such a thing. I reveled in the fact that I was alone. No eyes to watch me, no guards to hide my talents from. My body was tight from work and lack of proper use. A groan rattled in my throat as I stretched my tired legs.

Closing my eyes, I let my body fall into its natural rhythm. Letting the energy flow with my movements. I knew the movements were perfect. The Master who taught me saw to that. A wrong move earned you a cane to the back. When pain was a motivator, you learned fast. It also helped that my body naturally took to his training, as if my muscles knew the movements before my brain did. There were very few things I found myself not good at. Even now as I felt rusty, my body knew what to do.

Without opening my eyes, I targeted the punching bag I knew was hanging to the left of the mat. My movements changed from slow and controlled to powerful and precise. I could hear the bag protest as my skin connected with it. The connectivity was painful, but I took it in stride. Three months ago I would have felt nothing, but I had gone soft in my time here.

Suddenly, my senses flared and I knew I was no longer the only person in the room. He made no sound, but I knew he was here. I could feel the tension rising in my veins, a need to find release. As my senses opened up, it was like a floodgate. I could feel all of it now, every emotion I had stifled, every desire I had curbed. It was all there.

The suppressed rage I had for the man standing in the shadows, anger for letting myself get caught by The Subversive, repulsion for allowing myself to feel something other than hate for another human being, and fear… Somewhere buried in all of that rage and anger was fear. And I wanted nothing more than to extinguish it.

"I know you're there."

A slow applause echoed from the corner of the room.

"Impressive." Maddox's voice was cold as he stepped

from the shadows. "I wouldn't have pegged you for a fighter. You're so… small. Like I could *snap* you." He circled me like a prowling lion.

"Care to test that theory?" I glared at him. It was a reckless thing to say. I knew that. But my desire to lash out was stronger than my sense of reason at the moment.

His eyes glinted with pleasure in the dark light, but to my disappointment he didn't move.

"You're not scared of a little girl are you?"

That did it.

Stripping off his hoodie, he stepped into the ring and I immediately regretted my carelessness.

Here, we were on even ground. I was not trapped, locked in a shower room where no one could hear me scream. And I wasn't a prisoner any longer that he could torture without punishment. But even with all those things on my side, I was physically no match for him. His huge frame dominated mine. My only chance was to be faster.

Maddox's knuckles cracked as he flexed his meat-like hands. Taking my stance I prepared for his advance. The smug smile spreading across his lips sent a fire blazing though my mind and I lashed out first.

To my disappointment he was faster than he looked, but not fast enough. I landed a blow, catching him in the mouth. I grinned as I bounced backwards on the balls of my feet. A fine line of blood trickled down his chin.

Point, Phoenix.

Calmly, he wiped the blood from his lips and grinned at me. His advance came quickly. Each blow was calculated, packing shear force. I didn't have time to fight back. Instead, each movement was focused solely on blocking him. Each time his fists, knees or feet connected with my body, sharp pain flared with the impact, but I kept him at bay. Then there was an opening. A powerful thrust left his flank exposed and I attacked, throwing my elbow into his side. He staggered. I got three more blows in before he could recover. As my leg sprang out to deal a final blow his hands caught my calf. Apparently any sense of honorable fighting was now being thrown out. My body was suddenly airborne. I collided with something hard. My body bent, conforming to the shape of the punching bag before crashing to the floor.

I grimaced in pain as my lungs seized. Through the ringing in my ears I could hear him laughing. Tears burned in my eyes but I pushed them back.

"Ha!" I coughed, rolling to my feet. "The only way you can beat a poor little girl like me is to *cheat*."

"Cheat? Since when are there ever rules in Tartarus?"

"Tribesman through and through aren't you? Or maybe you are nothing but a born traitor." My head spun as I stood up. "Or better yet, maybe you're just an *inadequate* spy."

My gut clenched. I had gone too far. I could see something in him snap, the black of his eyes suddenly all consuming.

Moving with ferocity, Maddox ripped off his shirt exposing his bare chest. Tattoos covered every inch of his skin. Images of women burning in flames, skulls drowning in blackness and reapers hoisting dead bodies stared back at me. I recoiled from the pictures imprinted over his muscular chest, but he pressed himself closer. Maddox began to flick the underside of his tongue to me like a lizard— like it was supposed to mean something to me.

"Talented. Can you wipe your own ass too?" I snarled as my skin crawled.

He grabbed the front of my shirt and pulled me uncomfortably closer. "Do you see a mark?"

He flicked his tongue at me again. Repulsed, I pushed away shaking my head. "No. What's your point?"

"My point little girl, is that as high and mighty as you think you are, you know *nothing*. A *real* Taciturn spy bares only one mark on his body, a black star under his tongue. Which I plainly do not carry."

The woman consumed by the flames writhed as his

chest heaved beneath my nose.

"Good for you, so you're not a spy, that still proves nothing. I'm not even sure you actually left on your own. Maybe they kicked you out or maybe the relentless rejections from the women in your own Tribe weren't enough. You had to hear it from all of the others too."

His massive hands flashed out, the long fingers closing easily around my neck. He lifted until I could barely touch the ground, my toes just scraping the black mat.

"I watched the Tribe leader slaughter my *only* brother to set an example for those who disagreed with him. They slit his throat and skinned him while he was still alive. The Taciturn's leader now wears a vest of my brother's pelt as a reminder to those who think of standing against him." He squeezed tighter causing my vision to swim with blackness.

A hand shot out between us.

Triven was grabbing Maddox's forearm with surprising force, but his voice remained calm.

"Put the girl down Maddox."

He held me for a moment longer before finally letting go. Reflexively I coughed as the air burned back into my lungs. Triven's hand left a fading white imprint on Maddox's arm. His grasp must have been painful, but Maddox showed no sign of feeling it.

Carefully, I stepped around Triven, squaring my shoulders as I clutched my bruised neck.

I knew I should have felt pity for Maddox, apologized for what I had said. For the first time since we met I actually deserved his outrage. But despite that, I could only manage to return his icy glare.

"That doesn't change anything, I won't pity you." I hissed.

"Good thing I don't believe in pity." His dark eyes glittered as he loomed closer. I could smell his rank breath. A warmth filled me as Triven's chest pressed against my back, his hand on my shoulder ready to pull me away. With an unexpected and erratic laugh Maddox turned away and strode from the room.

That man definitely had a few screws loose.

***

I sucked in air as Triven pressed the cold compress to my neck. We were still in the training room.

"Sorry." He murmured. His thumb traced gingerly over the bruises. "These are going to look worse tomorrow."

"I know. Thank you… for coming after me tonight. You didn't have to step in like that. I could have handled him." I didn't quite meet his eyes. It was apparent to both of us I sucked at saying thank you.

"I know you could have." He was stroking my ego. We both knew I couldn't have taken Maddox. A few more seconds and I would have been unconscious. "I also know that you despise him and that tends to affect your judgment."

"It's not just that I despise him, it's that I don't trust him."

"He doesn't really give me the warm and fuzzies either, but he is a product of the world he was born into. Maddox wasn't raised like us. He never chose to be part of a Tribe. It was forced on him."

I thought of my own upbringing. I was born a child of The Sanctuary, but Tartarus raised me. And I was still a better person than he was. "I believe it's our choices that make us who we are and his certainly define him."

Triven was quiet for a while as he slowly nodded his head. "You're right. We may be handed a certain deck of cards but it is our choice how to play them. Maddox struggles with his inner demons every day, but remember, he *chose* to leave his Tribe and join us. His sins may be different from yours and mine, but we all sin."

He was right.

"Come on. We can still get a little sleep before

106

tomorrow." Triven dropped his hands from my neck and I followed him back to our room, feeling ashamed.

***

I never thought I would miss the wretched stench of Tartarus, but as the tainted air blew across my face I realized I did. It felt like so long since I felt outside air on my face, or saw the hazy night sky.

Triven shifted next to me. His ever-watchful eyes were, like mine, trained on the streets below us. Across the alley a shadow moved in the darkness. I knew Arden was just as restless as we were.

It was taking too long.

Archer and her team disappeared into the warehouse over thirty minutes ago and those of us left to stand guard were starting to get anxious. The day had passed in a blur. I couldn't remember eating or working or moving at all, but somehow I was now crouched on a rooftop surrounded by other unseen guards. I was the only one unarmed. Triven had fought for me saying I was an asset, that they could use my skills with a knife if not a gun. But Arstid wouldn't hear of it.

"Stay close by me at all times." Triven had murmured in my ear before we left.

I tugged idly at the fastenings on my vest. It was supposed to suppress body heat, to protect me, but I hated it. It felt awkward and heavy. Restraining.

"Leave it." Triven shot me a look as I pulled on the straps.

I scowled without looking at him, keeping my eyes on the street. "I did just fine without one of these things for six years, why do I need it now?"

"Humor me." He adjusted his gun on the roof's ledge.

I patted the rectangular shape hidden under my vest. My father's notebook was carefully concealed beneath the fold of restraining fabric. I had left Mouse with Veyron. At least I knew she would be in good hands, if I didn't return.

I had not yet decided if I wanted to return. My mind was still warring between freedom and staying. While trapped within the cement-lined walls of The Subversive headquarters, it was easier to stay. Seeing Mouse's innocent face, letting her tender brown eyes bore into mine made it impossible to leave her. But here, with the wind in my hair and the darkness of the night calling to me it was harder to want to go back.

When we had first emerged onto the streets I had thought about it. Barely a few seconds had passed before I had oriented myself and I knew running would be easy. I just needed the right moment. Leading the team to my roof access had been easy. I had even been impressed by how soundlessly we moved in such a large group. There were no lights on the street, and the green tinted clouds provided us with a perfect cover. When we had reached the alley, I took the rope from Triven and slung it over my shoulder without a thought. My fingers had easily found the familiar holds on the building's pocked surface, allowing me to scale two stories in less than thirty seconds. It wasn't until I had reached the railing and looked down that I realized this was it. This was the chance I had wanted, the moment that could lead to my freedom. The nine other bodies were waiting at the bottom for me to toss them the rope, but what if I didn't? I knew they couldn't follow me up the wall, not all of them anyway. I could have run. Mouse was in good hands; she would be safe under Triven's watch.

I could have run.

I could have, but I didn't. Instead I had tied off the rope and tossed it down.

Now waiting in this agonizingly crouched position I wondered if I had made a mistake, if I was a fool not to have run. I didn't get much of a chance to dwell on it though.

"They're out." Triven whispered as he pressed his eye to the scope.

There were five shadows moving across the warehouse

roof. We watched as they maneuvered over the beam balanced between the buildings. Once all ten feet were on solid ground we were in motion.

The team was scattered across the rooftops. Arden and Maddox were three roofs behind us, and closing in. Half of the team was already a block ahead of us and we had to gain some ground if we wanted to meet at the rendezvous point at the same time. Unlike some of The Subversive members, my feet were sure on the tarred surfaces. As we sprinted over the skyline, I could see them falling behind from the corner of my eye. Surprisingly, only Triven held his ground with me, his broad chest never far from my left shoulder. When I leapt from ledge to ledge his feet were nearly in sync with mine. A smile crept to my lips. It had been so long since I had moved like this, running at full tilt above the city. Triven's breathing next to me only heightened my ecstasy.

Ahead of us I could see the armored bodies disappear down the fire escape. Eager to beat Triven, I pushed my muscles harder. I could feel him pushing harder too. My smile widened, then abruptly fell. We were less than twenty feet from the ladder when the gunfire rang out from below.

13. TAMED

Screams echoed up the dilapidated walls, magnifying the sound. Chills splintered their way down my spine as the shrill human cries assaulted my ears. It sounded like a war was waging below us.

Six years of instinct kicked in and I skittered to a halt, the worn gravel rooftop sliding noisily under my feet. While my body halted, Triven's sped up. He glanced back for only a second before leaping over the edge of the building. Those were his people dying down there, his people in danger. But I didn't have people.

Did I?

I rushed to the roof's edge as Maddox and Arden caught up. Arden dove over the side landing on the fire escape. His feet had barely touched the rusted metal before he opened fire on the surging bodies below. Maddox spared one icy glare for me before joining the throng.

Bodies were strewn in the alley, but they weren't ours. Their skin was tainted odd colors. Taciturns.

We were surviving, not just surviving but winning. Every member of the guard was still on their feet. I leaned out further but didn't yet join the fight. Torn.

Run or help? Run… or stay?

I could see Triven moving below me, his sandy hair easily visible in the dark. He moved with a perilous grace. Without shedding a bullet or unsheathing a knife, he advanced like a shadow through the alley, debilitating the Tribesman as he went. It took me a moment to realize he wasn't killing them; he was just rendering them unconscious. He moved with perfect precision. It seemed as if he saw everything around him all at one, everything but *one* man.

But I saw him.

As the tattooed arm rose, the glint of the black blade flashed in the night. There was no mistaking his target. The man's eyes were on Triven.

I didn't hesitate.

Launching myself from the ledge, I grabbed the fire escape railing. My hands caught for only a second, allowing me to better my aim. I dropped once more, letting two stories fall past, my hands recalculating on the next landing. Then just as quickly as before, I let go and dropped the last fifteen feet.

I could feel the man's bones break as my feet landed on his back. The muscular body crumpled beneath me, absorbing the full impact of my fall. Triven turned in shock as I crashed down beside him. Two seconds later and there would have been a knife in his back. I wanted to keep looking into those hazel eyes, but there was no time.

Taciturns mobbed us. Everywhere I turned, tattooed bodies appeared, their weapons slashing, firing and stabbing.

Fear shut off and the instinctual animal within me was unleashed.

It took me less than three seconds to disarm an attacker and turn her weapon back on her. In another three seconds, I had a knife for my left hand and another two Taciturns lay at me feet. A gun fired somewhere near my head and I had to blink to keep my vision clear. The ringing in my ear deafened all of the other sounds in the alley. I blinked again as I struggled to find focus. There was something fuzzy coming into focus at the back of the alley. A girl was pinned to the ground with a Taciturn male over her, but she was not fighting back. Her head lolled to the side as she struggled for consciousness. I recognized the dark curly hair. Archer. The man sat astride her as his fingers traveled over her chest, the other hand pressed a knife to her throat.

I could feel a strand of sanity within me snap, and my vision went red. The knife left my hand instantly, and even as it lodged into his side I charged. I was on him before he could react. My weapons were forgotten as my fists collided over and over with his face. I knew he wasn't one of the men who had raped my mother, he wasn't Maddox leering at my naked body in the showers, but at that moment, he was. He was all of those things. I punched until his face was no longer recognizable.

A large hand grabbed my shoulder and spun me. I thrust to kill, and froze. My knife stopped at the assailant's throat, a thick trickle of blood running from beneath the blade.

Triven stood frozen, his gentle eyes wide but calm as they watched me. The knife fell from my hand. It sounded so loud as it clattered to the ground.

"I'm sorry." I said in a trembling voice. My body began to shake, but I didn't feel cold.

"Phoenix." Triven whispered my name as he moved towards me, but I jumped backwards.

"I'm sorry." I shook my head, my eyes widening. I had lost control... I had almost killed him.

He moved towards me again and this time I did not move. His muscular arms wrapped around me, and despite myself, I fell against his chest.

"I'm sorry." Why couldn't I find any other words?

He smoothed my hair, "It's okay. We're okay. We have to get moving though, it isn't safe."

I nodded as he released me. Following his lead, I took Archer under the arm and we moved back towards the door leading to The Subversive bunker.

***

There were minor injuries— a few bullet grazes, a couple shallow knife wounds and Archer had a concussion— but overall we had been very fortunate. The reconnaissance mission hadn't been a complete waste. The access to The Sanctuary was definitely not on the premises, but Archer's team had found a surprise stash of Sanctuary-grade weaponry in the warehouse. Technology that advanced had definitely not come from Tartarus. There was a surplus of heat-seeking guns, titanium knives, motion sensor bombs and lightweight body armor. While we didn't find the entrance to The Sanctuary, we did find proof that someone was smuggling weapons out to the Ravagers. And if there was a way to get weapons out, then there was a way to get in.

Once we were back inside I avoided everyone. I helped get Archer to Doc Porters and then slipped out during the chaos. I felt Triven's eyes on me as I left, but I didn't stop. I couldn't even bear to find Mouse, to tell her I was okay, because I wasn't. I couldn't look at her innocent face after what I had done. Not yet anyway.

There was still blood on my hands. Some of it was my own, but the rest was a morbid reminder of what I had just done. I practically ran to the shower room, eager to wash the evidence from my skin, to shed my tainted clothing and hide behind the locked door.

I stood in the shower until it turned cold and even then I couldn't shake the sickness rolling through my stomach. I had scrubbed at my hands until they were raw. The Taciturns' blood had long since washed off, now only my own tinted the water as I ran the soap over my raw skin. My knuckles were bruised and split, but I continued to scrub until they burned. I had never lost control before, never forgotten who I was, but tonight I did. And it had almost cost Triven his life. The person I had leapt from a building to save, nearly died at my own hand in my blinded rage.

When I finally emerged from the shower room— with the feeling of death still on my skin— there was a figure leaning against the wall waiting for me. She was moving, slower than usual, her dark eyes still slightly unfocused. I hovered in the doorway watching her.

Archer hesitated, "Um... Triven told me what you did."

I cringed. Waiting for her wrath. I deserved it. I had almost killed him.

"I am in your debt. Thank you for saving my life." She couldn't meet my eyes.

That was not what I had been expecting.

"Oh... It was nothing really." I had saved Archer, but for the first time in my life I ended another's out of rage, not self-defense. I felt sick again.

"Mmm, yeah... well I owe you one. And I pay my debts." She shifted her weight uneasily. Relying on others was obviously not easy for her either. "Are you headed to the party?"

"Party?" I stared blankly at her. What could we possibly have to celebrate?

"We usually have a gathering after every recon mission. When a member dies we gather to mourn. When we all return home, we celebrate life." Archer's eyes lit on mine for a brief second. "This is the first time we have been able to celebrate in a while."

I nodded, understanding her. She had come very close to being mourned tonight. Before I could refuse, she wrapped her thin hand over the crook of my elbow for support. I flinched, which made her smile. She was so much taller and more beautiful than me. While we were about the same age, I must have looked like a child next to her.

"The choice to go is yours, but if I'm being honest, I could use a hand getting there. The floor still seems to tilt at odd angles if I move my head too fast."

I surprised myself by smiling back at her. "Lead the

way."

The celebration was being held in the dining hall. Tables had been pushed to the walls and the lights dimmed. People were gathered throughout the room. I could see other members from our mission scattered among the groups. People were clapping them on the backs, hugging them. Several residents had makeshift instruments and were playing music in the corner. Spirits seemed high. Then, someone saw us. Cheers erupted from the crowd as faces turned in our direction. Archer let go of my arm and I let her walk forward to her people. I turned to leave, but other hands found me. A few brave souls patted me on the shoulders while drawing me into the room. Most people just shared warm smiles and inclined heads as I passed.

It was a strange feeling. I was not one of them, yet they were welcoming me. Well, most of them were. Arstid stood like a porcelain statue in the back corner of the room. The bald-headed Willets was at her side.

She knew.

She knew I had lost control and almost killed one of her best soldiers. As her frosty glare held mine, a small body collided with me, tearing my attention away.

Mouse wrapped her arms around my waist, hugging me as hard as her tiny arms could. It felt good. I hugged her back, pressing my cheek to her head. I had to be better, if not for myself than for her. When she pulled away I felt a little hollow.

Mouse reached up pressing her palms to my face. Her round face was elated as she gazed at me. Then, grabbing my hand she pressed it to her cheek as she grinned.

"I missed you too." I whispered and Mouse's brown eyes sparkled.

She pulled me away from the crowd to the corner of the room where a man stood. His back was turned to us, but I knew how beautiful his face was. How caring his eyes were. I also knew there would be a small cut just below his right ear.

My chest tightened.

Before I could pull back, Mouse touched his hand. I expected hate in his eyes when they saw me, but instead there was something else. Relief maybe? He smiled at me before turning back to Mouse.

"Thank you for finding her." He cupped her face. "I was beginning to think Archer had decided she wasn't so grateful after all."

Triven smiled warmly at me and some of the tension in my chest released. He didn't hate me. I could feel a strange heat rising in my cheeks. I wished he would look away and then again I didn't. Mouse bounced on the balls of her feet as her head swiveled between the two of us.

Something small, bouncy and blonde broke the awkward moment. A girl no bigger than Mouse pounced between us. Her golden ringlets fell in a striking disarray, her brilliantly blue eyes startling as she glanced up at me.

"See! I told you she would be fine." She addressed Mouse in a high but overly loud voice. "Mouse here was worried you wouldn't come back, but I told her she was just over-reacting. Tough girls like you always come back. I mean look at Archer."

Her words rolled out in such a blur that it took my mind a minute to catch up. Mouse reached out, taking the bouncing blonde's hand as she smiled at me. She had a friend. I smiled at the loud little blonde.

"I'm Phoenix." I said, trying to set a good impression for Mouse's first friend.

"I know." She said swinging her arms. "Pretty much everybody knows who you are."

I glanced up at Triven, but he just grinned and shrugged his shoulders.

"*My* name is Maribel. Everybody says I talk too much, but Mouse doesn't seem to mind. And since she doesn't talk at all, I figure I speak enough for the both of us."

Mouse grinned at her nodding. It was obvious she had found a mouthpiece and was elated by her new friend.

"Veyron said there's cake. Want to go find out what kind?" Maribel's eyes lit with mischief. Mouse nodded and the two disappeared into the crowd, leaving Triven and I alone.

I smiled shyly at him, but then my eyes flickered to the cut on his neck and I felt myself pale. My fault. A boisterous laugh interrupted my guilty musings and Arden appeared with two bottles in his hands.

"You two look like you could use these." He thrust a bottle into each of our hands. "Cook brewed up a new batch this week, fair warning this stuff is potent."

He laughed again as I took a whiff and wrinkled my nose. Someone called Arden's name and we were alone again. I stared at the amber liquid.

"I was worried about you." Triven swirled the bottle in his hand.

I took a big swig and nearly choked, my eyes, throat and nose were all on fire. A shudder roared through my body in response. Triven laughed, as my eyes watered.

"He wasn't kidding." I sputtered. It took me a moment to catch my breath.

"Go easy on that stuff. Cook's home brews can knock you flat if you drink too fast." Triven sipped at his as if it were merely water.

"I'm sorry about earlier." I murmured.

"Don't." His eyes were tight as they turned on me. "Don't apologize anymore. You saved Archer's life. You saved mine. These people would be mourning tonight if it hadn't been for you."

The back of his hand brushed my cheek. Surprising us both, I didn't flinch away. A warm flush crept to my cheeks. I fervently hoped most people would think it was just from the alcohol. The music picked up and people began to dance. I shifted, moving closer to Triven, feeling the icy wall between us melt.

As Cook's liquor was passed around, more people had begun to dance and the flush in my cheeks deepened. Mouse

117

and Maribel had found the cake and the two were now sharing a piece as they played some kind of hand game.

"How do you do it?"

"Do what?" Triven's head swiveled towards me as we sat on a table against the wall.

"Care about someone. Deal with the constant worry that every day something could take them from you." I watched Mouse as she laughed when Maribel missed her hand.

"One day at a time. Mostly you learn to cherish those moments that are good. Like these. Nothing in the world is permanent, so you have to make those good moments count."

I could feel his eyes on me.

"And when everything falls apart?"

"Then you lean on those who will help you pick up the pieces."

I nodded as Maribel whispered something to Mouse. Both pairs of mischievous eyes turned our way. Mouse managed to drag Triven to the makeshift dance floor as I watched from my seat, still sipping the amber concoction slowly. Triven twirled her as she laughed. For the first time since I met her, she looked like a carefree child. At that moment, I wanted nothing more than to keep her that way. To let her be happy. As they danced, something snow white caught my eye. Arstid was standing near the door. She and Willets had their heads bent low, discussing something in hushed tones. Something was going on. As Arstid slipped though the doors, several other men I recognized as guards followed her. I craned my neck watching them. I thought about following but something blocked my view.

Mouse appeared in front of me grinning. She had left Triven to dance with the bouncing Maribel. I tried to shoo her hands as they pulled at me, but eventually I could no longer resist her silent pleading. I wasn't sure if it was Cook's brew or the happy atmosphere, but I allowed her to lead me to the dance floor. I spun Mouse barely three times before she pulled away, reaching again for Maribel's hand, and the two twirled away leaving Triven and I standing alone in a crowd of people.

Just as I stepped back to retreat, Triven's hand pressed against the small of my back. My hands fell against his chest as he pulled me close. Our cheeks pressed together as his mouth found my ear. His skin felt pleasantly hot against my own.

"I think we were just set up by two diabolical little girls."

I giggled.

I giggled. It felt strange even as it came out.

"I think you're right."

"Well let's not disappoint them."

Before I could speak, Triven's hand gathered mine and we began to dance. Correction— he began to dance, I was just along for the ride. He moved as if I weighed nothing, my feet barely seeming to touch the ground as we turned and glided along. Before I knew it, I was laughing. Triven's returning husky laugh was warm against my ear. The song ended and the crowd began to cheer for the band. While we had stopped moving, my head was still spinning. I pressed my face to his broad shoulder to steady it. He smelled like soap and spices.

"Do you want to leave?" He whispered in my ear. He was winded, his words coming out airy. The deep sultry tone of his voice stirred something inside of me— I was sure it was Cook's brew that had lowered my usually steeled walls. I looked up into those perfect eyes and nodded. His returning smile could have melted stone.

The hallways seemed to pass in a blur as I followed him. I stared, mesmerized by my hand in his. Less than a month ago, I wouldn't have let anyone touch me, much less as a sign of affection. But it felt good, he felt good. We made it back to our room without passing anyone. It seemed everyone was at the celebration tonight. Triven held the door open for me and I could barely meet his eyes as I brushed past his chest. When the door clanked shut, I froze.

What was I doing? This was a bad idea. Getting attached to another person could only cause me more pain. I knew all of that but I still wanted this. Every cell in my body wanted this. It had taken Cook's brew to allow me to be honest with myself, and now I finally realized what I had been so vehemently denying. I wanted him.

Triven's warm fingers traveled over my bare shoulders, causing me to shiver. I turned to face him. His hazel eyes were like warm honey and his lips were flushed. My heart began to race as his hands continued to brush over my arms.

"This isn't a good idea." I said staring at his lips.

His hands moved to my jaw, sliding across the slender bones to the nape of my neck.

"Triven…" I whispered. I was trying to warn him. I wasn't a good choice. I was broken, damaged goods. He deserved better than what I could offer him. He deserved more than what I was. I was too hollow, too ruined.

He lowered his face to mine and I sucked in a scared breath. He stopped, his lips inches from mine. His eyes scanned my face, but he didn't move. We stayed like this for what felt like an eternity. His breath was warm and sweet on my face. I knew what he was doing. Even in his state of lowered inhibitions, he wasn't going to move. He was waiting for me to make the last move, telling me it was my choice.

Push him away. My mind screamed. I knew this was a bad idea, that it would only lead to pain. *Push him away!* I pressed my palms to his chest, ready to shove him away but my heart rebelled. Moving with the speed of desperation, I clutched him and pressed my lips to his.

14. SELFISH

His lips fit seamlessly with mine. As my mouth pressed feverishly against his, he reciprocated with a ferocity that made me purr. He wanted me just as I wanted him, maybe even more. As his hands moved against my body, a tingling sensation spread over my skin like wildfire. Every part of my body lit like a struck match. My mind wheeled and my heart ignited. And I felt something for the first time, something other than hate or fear or guilt. I felt alive.

Somehow, we made our way to the bed. Triven was careful to keep me on top, to let me stay in control. While his hands firmly held me, I knew he would stop the second I asked him to. Only I didn't ask.

We lay pressed together, mouths moving in unison until we couldn't breathe. When I finally pulled away, gasping for air, his lips trailed my jaw before resting next to my ear. We laid in silence listening to each other's breathing. Beneath me Triven's heart hammered against his chest.

My lips grazed the cut on his neck and the guilt came back. Carefully I ran my finger over the healing skin. Then surprising myself, I kissed it. Triven's arms closed around me.

"I thought you were going to run." He whispered in my

ear. There was pain in his voice, as if the idea hurt him. "When you were standing on the fire escape. There was this look in your eyes and I thought you were going to run."

I pressed my ear to his chest. "I was going to. At least I thought I was going to."

He ran his hand through my hair. "I'm glad you didn't."

I was silent. I was glad I stayed too. Wasn't I?

His fingers sought mine, the pads running over my bruised and raw knuckles. Even his gentle touch stung. I balled them into fists, ashamed of what I had done. He pressed his cheek to my forehead, closing his hand protectively over mine.

"Phoenix, what you did… it was—"

"Dishonorable," I cut him off. "I lost control. I felt like… like I lost who I was. When I saw that man on top of Archer, I just snapped. It was like watching my mother… I have never lost control like that. Never. I mean, I have killed people before— I'm not proud of it— but it was always a kill or be killed situation. But tonight… I… I… Then I turned on you." I buried my face in his chest. "Triven I never meant to hurt you. I would never… And my parents, what if Arstid is right? What if they were the cause of your father's death? You should hate me Triven. You should want me to suffer for what they've done. For what *I* have done. I am not a good person. Why did you save me Triven, why didn't you just let me die in that alley?"

The words began to pour out and I couldn't stop them. They had been eating away at me. He just held me tighter and let me sputter out on my own. Once my breathing calmed he spoke.

"We have all done things we're not proud of. None of us are murderers by nature and no one could ever blame you for what you did. We have grown up in a world filled with hate and violence, and it's bound to seep in eventually. You are *not* a bad person Phoenix; you are a product of the world that raised you. But the pain you feel proves that you are still a good person, that you have held on to your humanity. My father died saving my life, but that is in the past. I can't change it. Even if your parents did set his death in motion, you are not them. You may be a product of your parents, but they're not who *you* are. Too many people get caught up in the past. If we keep punishing people for what their parents or their ancestors have done, the world as a whole can never move forward. Society will never grow. With time, open wounds only fester, better to let them heal and forgive than to fester with hate."

He was right. A part of me knew he was right, but I still didn't feel worthy of his forgiveness— or of Mouse's trust. Both of these righteous, kind people trusted me, but I barely trusted myself. I had put all of my faith in my parents, but what if I had been wrong to do so? What if they were everything Arstid claimed they were? I was angry at her for poking a hole in the fragile bubble that was my world. I was angry with my parents for leaving me alone here. And I was angry with myself for questioning them and for *not* questioning them sooner.

"Do you want me to leave?" Triven whispered. I could only just detect the pain in his voice.

Yes.

"No."

I don't know…

We laid in silence for a while as his words swirled though my mind. The moment of passion between us was gone, but his body still felt good next to mine.

"Mouse will be coming soon." I said.

"She is staying with Maribel tonight." He paused. "I hope that's okay, I thought it would be good for her to spend time with children her own age."

"I think that's a good idea." I was not the role model she needed; more time with normal undamaged people was good for her. I rolled away from him. Triven would be better off away from me too. But as my body moved from his, he followed. His arm draped over me as his breath tickled my ear. I should have pushed him away, but I didn't want to. It was selfish, I knew that. I would only hurt him, but I wanted him here. My lips still tingled from where he had kissed me and despite every logical part of my brain, I liked it.

"Why *did* you save me, Triven?" I kept my back to him. It was easier to talk when I didn't have to look into his eyes.

"The night I saved you in the alley, it wasn't the first time I saw you."

I stared hard at the metal door, trying to keep my voice calm. "What do you mean it wasn't the first time you saw me?"

I could feel his wince. "I had gone to pick up new books for my collection and while I was gathering some books on history, a girl dropped down out of the ceiling vent."

I flushed with anger at myself. How had I not realized he was there?

"You moved nearly as silently as I did. At first I thought you were a Tribesman, but you showed no signs of belonging to any Tribe. The longer I watched you, the more I began to realize you were a rogue. At first I thought you had come looking for books to burn. I thought about stopping you, but then I realized you were reading them. I had never met another person outside of The Subversive who could read. I was about to approach you when the Ravagers showed up." Anger singed his tone. "I saw them before you did, but there was no way to warn you. Instead I led them away. By the time I returned you had disappeared."

"I never even knew you were there." I admitted. I was now indebted to him twice.

"I know." He sounded a little smug. "Then that night I found you again. When I realized you were the one in the alley saving the little girl… I had never seen anyone like you. You were utterly captivating. But we weren't fast enough. At first I thought we were too late, that I would never get to meet the girl who had so quickly stolen my heart, but then you woke up."

I thought back on all of the times Triven had watched me, each time he had defended me and trusted me. While I had been looking at him for any sign of deception, he had been looking for love. My chest tightened. I wasn't capable of love, was I? I had read about it, dreamt about it even, but it was a wasted emotion that only caused pain and heartache. But as Triven's chest rose and fell against me, I felt something. What though, I wasn't sure.

Cook's drink was still heavy in my system and I was finding it hard to keep my eyes open. Triven's breathing had grown deeper as well.

"What's your real name?" His words slurred a little with sleep.

I had never told anyone this, no one living remembered who I was before I became Phoenix. Arstid knew my parents, but even she knew no details from my past. I waited two heartbeats as I thought and he retracted his question.

"Never mind, sorry to ask. I understand you don't want to talk about it. Can you tell me why you picked the name Phoenix though?" He stifled a yawn. "It seems to suit you."

"When my parents died, I was only eleven. I saw the whole thing happen, my mother's rape, both of my parent's brutal murders. I remember biting my hand so hard I nearly gagged on my own blood. I wanted to die with them. To forget everything I had just seen. But my mother had told me to survive and I couldn't bear to let her last words be forgotten. When I finally got out of the storm drain, I realized a large part of me died in that alley with my parents. Maybe that's why I remember so little of my life before then. Their sweet eleven-year-old child no longer existed. And I was what rose from her ashes." I swallowed thickly.

"It's the perfect name." Triven's breath warmed my ear. He no longer sounded sleepy. I shuddered, not knowing if it was from being cold or from dredging up old memories. Reflexively, I pressed my back farther into him seeking a comfort that I'd never known before. His arm wrapped over me, anchoring me to him like a safety line.

We lay in silence as the weight of the day dragged us into the world of sleep. Just before I drifted away, I offered him something I hadn't given to anyone before, the last piece of my old self I had left. As I whispered in the darkness I could feel sleep taking me. But before I succumbed, I heard the sound of my name as he repeated it. It was a name no one had spoken in six years, and a shiver ran down my spine.

"Prea."

***

A loud banging woke me, jolting me from my dreams. It took me a moment to remember where I was. Something heavy was draped over my body.

The banging vibrated the room and suddenly the pressure on my body was gone. Triven moved swiftly to the door, holding up a finger asking me stay put.

What time was it? How long had we been asleep?

Archer stood in the dim hallway, her eyes uncharacteristically wide with fear. There was blood on her shirt.

I jumped to my feet as Triven's shoulders tensed. Something was wrong.

"What happened?" His voice was deep, commanding.

"There was a second recon mission. They were meant to retrieve some of the weapons we discovered." She shook her head, unable to meet our eyes. "The Ravagers ambushed us, two dead and four injured."

"Who?" Triven's hands were clenching and unclenching at his sides.

"Marks and Weaver." Archer stared at his chest. It was the first time I had seen her look ashamed. It made the hairs on my neck stand up.

"Why wasn't I informed of this?" The tone in his voice sent chills down my spine. This was not the voice of the gentle man I had shared a bed with last night. This was the voice of a military leader.

"The orders came from above, you were not to be

involved." Her eyes flitted to me.

I was not to be involved. That's what she meant. Apparently Arstid's distrust for me had only matured with time. Triven was not informed because of me. He didn't miss this either. Grabbing my wrist he pushed past Archer, pulling me with him. She looked hurt and ashamed as I glanced back at her. Triven moved with surprising speed through the halls. My usually nimble feet were struggling to keep up. Stragglers from last night's celebration still lingered in the halls, their curious eyes following our hurried progression. They didn't know yet.

We paused outside of the doors that led to the round-tabled meeting room. Voices were carrying through the door, but they were too muffled to understand. Only the volume gave away that it was a heated conversation. Triven's shoulders heaved as he took a deep breath, his hand tightened on mine. As I looked at our intertwined fingers, a dawning realization came over me. For the first night in six years, my parents' murders hadn't haunted my dreams. I had awoken in Triven's arms not because of my muffled screams but because of something else.

Before I could speak, before I could think any more about it, we were through the doors. The conversation stopped the instant we walked in. Arstid stood in front of her usual chair with her palms pressed to the table. Her face was flushed, her usually perfect hair falling around her face in a random array of white. Maddox stood across from her with Willets and the blonde guard whose name I still didn't remember. As her eyes fell on my hand in Triven's, her face tightened. I loosened my grip, but he only constricted his in response.

"Who ordered the mission tonight?" Triven's voice was like ice. Suddenly no one could meet his eyes, not even Arstid.

"We made the decision without you. It was decided that your judgment might be recently impaired—" Arstid stammered.

"Impaired?" Triven's voice rose. "The only judgment that seems to be impaired is yours, *Mother*. Since when have we

127

ever sent out a team without the input of the entire council?"

The word mother was like a slap in the face. Why hadn't I seen it before? Triven wasn't just a well-spoken youth his peers looked up to. He was the heir to The Subversive. Every glare Arstid threw our way, every time Maddox had backed down from a fight now made sense. I should have been angry that he never told me, but in all fairness I never asked. I also understood him enough now to know it wasn't about lying to me about who his mother was, it was about being seen as a man within the community and not just their leader's son. While I stared with enlightenment at Arstid and Triven, the others shamefully averted their eyes.

"You sent our men out, without our best team to protect them, without the proper planning and look what it has cost us! Your stubborn prejudice has cost two of our own their lives. And for what?! Weapons we don't need? All because you can't see past your own hate? There will be no more missions without the full council's knowledge, do you understand? You are our leader, *not* our ruler and you would do well to remember that."

Arstid paled. I couldn't tell if it was from anger or because her only son had just pulled rank on her.

"Everyone out, I need to speak to my son alone." Her usually strong voice quavered.

The other members of the guard did not hesitate. As I turned to follow them out, Triven's hand tightened on mine. "Phoenix stays."

Arstid's lips whitened to match her face, disappearing into a thin line.

She seethed, glaring at me. "I was foolish enough to trust her mother, I will not be the fool twice. This is all their fault! Her parents lead us here, lead your father to his—"

I cut her off.

"It's easy to blame the dead, isn't it? Seeing as how they can't defend themselves." My words were harsh, malice coating every syllable. A twisted pleasure blossomed as I watched the words slap Arstid's face. But even with that pleasure, a seed of doubt was still infiltrating my mind. *What if she was right?*

A spasm of pain flickered across Triven's face.

I took a deep breath and pressed my palm to his arm. "It's okay, I'll go."

He nodded at me and to both Arstid's shock and mine, he pressed his lips to my forehead before releasing my hand. As soon as the door closed behind me I was in motion. I bolted down the empty hall and darted into a cleaning closet I had seen once before. Scaling the shelves with familiar ease, I pressed against the air vent. Relief washed over me as it gave way and I slipped inside. Though it had been nearly two months since I had been in an airshaft, years of practiced movement rekindled instantly. I moved quickly and silently through the dust coated metal. Triven's deep voiced carried through the shaft giving me guidance. In less than a minute I was hovering above the round table watching Arstid's snow-white head through the slits.

"How dare you undermine me in front of—"

Triven interrupted her. "I was simply reminding you of what you seemed to have forgotten. We are not a Tribe, Mother, nor are we part of The Sanctuary. Years ago, it was agreed that we would be a democracy of equals. You were the one who pushed so hard for that. Or have you forgotten what you and Dad sacrificed so much for?"

She recoiled, stung before lashing back. "Do *not* bring your father up to me. Of course I know what I sacrificed for. Sometimes I think you are the one who forgets. You were too young to remember, too young to understand—"

"But I'm not too young now." His tone softened a little. "I am not a child anymore. I am a peer, a leader in this community and you owe me that respect."

She scoffed and sank into her chair. "Respect? Please. You can barely see past your own nose these days. That impetuous little street brat has you so wrapped up you can't see what is good for yourself much less your own people any more.

129

I know what happened in the alley. She may have saved Archer but that rage she possesses makes her a threat. Phoenix is like a wild dog, Triven. She may turn on you at any moment. It is foolish to trust her."

Pain stabbed my heart. She was right.

"Then I am a fool." Triven's words only drove the knife deeper.

"She can't stay here." Arstid's voice wavered as she pinched the bridge of her nose.

"If she goes, I go. She needs us even if she doesn't know it yet. She needs our help as much as we need hers." His voice was still strong.

"Triven…" Arstid faltered and he went in for the kill.

"We promised we would help all those in need. By your own creed she has the right to be here just as much as the rest of us. She may look like her mother to you but she is not. Phoenix is a different person. The only one who can't see that is you. She stays or we both go."

I retreated from my hiding place as their voices continued. I didn't want to hear anymore. I couldn't stand to hear the trust in Triven's voice any longer, the compassion. He was wrong and for the first time Arstid and I agreed. I was a danger to him. Why couldn't he see that? Despite his amorous words, a prideful anger built in me. I didn't need them. I didn't need to stay here with them, to be protected by their walls and charitable handouts. I had survived by myself for six years. Screw them for thinking I needed them. I needed no one.

I pushed past people in the halls as I made my way back to our room. I made eye contact with no one, all niceties gone. It didn't matter. My hands flew over my few belongings, stuffing everything unceremoniously into my tattered bag. In my haste I dropped my father's pocket watch and it bounced under the bed. Cursing, I dropped to my knees. As my fingertips searched, I came across something stuffed under the corner of the bed. I grabbed it, along with the familiar chain of my watch and yanked. My heart sputtered.

It was a small piece of paper with a child's drawing on it. Three scribbled figures were smiling up at me. Mouse had drawn a picture of us. A little girl stood in the middle holding hands with a taller blonde girl and a tall sandy haired boy with hazel eyes. The word family was scrawled beneath it. My eyes burned.

"I assume you heard most of our conversation."

I hadn't heard him come in, but he was standing in the doorway watching me. His warm eyes waited as he leaned against the doorframe. I crumpled the drawing and shoved it into the backpack with my other things.

"Please don't leave." He whispered. My heart ripped as I kept my back to him. "I should have told you sooner that Arstid was my mother, but I didn't want you to see me as nothing more than her son. Besides, she stopped being my mother years ago. I don't agree with her about any of it. She's wrong."

I shook my head.

"She's right. I am a danger to all of you. I'm not good at working with others, you said it yourself. I'm not loyal to anyone." I kept putting things in my bag, ignoring the pain growing in my chest. I turned to leave and ran into his chest.

"Move." I said staring at his shoulder.

"No."

"*Move.*"

"No."

I could feel the rage building in me. Why was he being so stubborn? Why couldn't he see how wrong I was for him? For everyone here? They would all be better off without me, even Mouse. I wanted them. I knew that now. I wanted people to love me. The drawing crumpled in my bag proved that. I *wanted* them, but I didn't *need* them.

"I don't need you, you know. Despite what you said to Arstid I don't *need* your help. I don't need anyone." I hoped the words would sting, that he would finally feel hurt and let me go. Last night had been a mistake. I had let him get too close. I

131

stepped to the side but he moved with me.

"I know, Prea." He whispered my name and I froze, teetering on my thin emotional ledge. "I know that you don't need me, but I need you. Despite what Arstid says *we* need you."

My shoulders began to sag and he pressed on, taking advantage of my weakness. "You are strong and fearless and the kind of person we need on our side. If you won't stay for me, then stay for her. Mouse will be lost without you. She needs you. Without you she is just another child abandoned in Tartarus."

That was a low blow.

I pressed my head to his shoulder. I wanted to stay. I should leave. I wanted Mouse to be safe, to have the life I didn't. I didn't want her to be like me, but I didn't want to abandon her like my parents had done to me.

"For her." I said closing my eyes as I let Triven take the bag from my shoulder.

15. DIPLOMACIES

I pressed my fingers to my temples. My head was pounding as the voices blurred around me. We had spent another day trapped in the meeting room listening to the council members squabble with one another. Since the botched acquisition mission, faith in Arstid's leadership seemed to falter. Odder still, people were starting to listen to me. A plan had been set in motion before I joined their little assembly, but without a way into The Sanctuary it had come to a screeching halt. To most of the council involved, it felt like a setback, but to me it seemed like an opportunity.

The Subversive had spent the last six years recruiting fallen Tribesman and training them. They now knew the inside workings of every Tribe, every Tribe but one. The one I wanted to see fall more than any other. The one I seemed to know the most about. Who knew all of my vengeful thieving would actually yield something other than vindictive gratification.

There was no question now that the Ravagers had a link to The Sanctuary. The question now was were they merely stealing or was The Sanctuary supporting them? Those hotheaded members like Archer and Maddox needed no further proof than the weapons we discovered and wanted to launch a blind attack on the Ravagers. They felt the best way to wage a war was to pull the trigger first. Others, like Veyron and Willets, reverted back to their Adroit roots and sought more information before wanting to get their hands dirty. They felt a war was best started with knowledge and a strategy. The resulting disagreement was what made my head hurt.

Everyone's head swiveled to me. Someone had just asked me a question, but I wasn't listening.

"What do you think?" Arden raised his eyebrows, awaiting my answer. Instead of admitting my inattention, I spoke the thoughts running through my own mind.

"Bickering about this isn't getting us anywhere. We don't have enough information to act but we can't just sit around waiting for something to happen. The Ravagers may be Id-driven monsters, but they are not fools. They must know we are moving against them now. It's not just them either. Something in the city is changing. All of the Tribes have become restless. That attack the other night in the alley was no coincidence. You are not as invisible as you used to be. The Tribes know you're here and they won't let you slip by unscathed. You are a band of deserters and miscreants to them. If you think you have seen their wrath, you haven't seen anything yet. If they catch up to you, pray you are killed and not captured.

"With that said, I think we need to split off into small groups, bring less attention to ourselves. There's safety in numbers, but not when you are trying to keep a low profile. Teams of two or three need to start scouting the city, watching the Tribes' movements. I have a few allies outside of the Tribes that I can call on. The time has come to take action. I have safe houses located throughout the city that are conveniently located near the Tribes' dens. I suggest we use them."

"You mean stay out there?" Willets looked at me with blatant disbelief.

"Yes. Hiding in here will yield you nothing. If you want a revolution then you need to start acting like soldiers. Thieving weapons will only get you so far. It's time you started using them or the Tribes will continue to pick us off one by one. You need to start not only fighting back, but also picking the fights. The key is turning them against each other. Tensions between the Tribes are already at a breaking point, we just need to give them the final push."

Archer perked up. "You mean setting up other Tribes for our attacks?"

"No one knows better than you how the Wraiths fight, who better to falsify one of their attacks than a former Tribesman?"

"I won't murder people. I am not like *them*." Archer bristled.

"I'm not asking you to murder anyone. I am saying destroy some food supplies, burn a few vacant meeting locations, and leave marks on claimed territories. It doesn't take a death to frame another Tribe."

"And while the Tribes war with one another, the Ravagers will be easier to infiltrate." Triven followed my train of thought.

"Exactly." I nodded at him.

A murmur of appreciation filtered through the room. Only Arstid remained frozen as she avoided my eyes. I could hear the plans begin to emerge as they spoke. Old Tribesmen leaned into one another, comparing their thoughts. The few survivors from The Sanctuary looked slightly lost as their counterparts interacted.

"All those in favor?" Triven's voice carried over the din.

"Aye!" Over half of the room shouted in unison.

We had a plan.

***

Mouse's eyes blurred with tears, but she didn't let a single one fall. Triven and I had packed for four days. Several of our elected groups were already spread throughout the city, wreaking havoc on the tainted citizens of Tartarus. Our plan was working. Tribes were beginning to attack each other. And with my knowledge of the Ravagers, many of the Tribe wars were effectively blamed on them. It seemed an uprising was indeed brewing and it smelled like revolution. The other members of The Subversive had done their part, now it was our turn.

Triven and I were to gather information. I had a few allies in the outside world that could prove useful. There was one in particular I needed to speak to, but trust was not something you could earn from him. In my pack I carried three titanium knives, a heat-seeking gun and a motion-sensor bomb. They were most of what the ambushed recon party had stolen from the Ravagers. They seemed heavy in my pack. Their weight was a constant reminder that I had not confided their presence to Triven. Mouse's drawing was also stuffed in my bag as a reminder to come back. It bothered me that such a sweet drawing was currently pressed against a lethal bomb. That alone was a sick reminder why I was doing this.

Mouse held my hand as we moved towards one of the escape hatches. She knew we would be gone for a few days and I could see the fear in her eyes that she understood we might not come back. To be honest, that thought scared me too. As I glanced down at the orphaned child holding my hand, it still shocked me how much she had changed my life. When we reached the door I crouched down to her level, taking her hands in mine.

"We will be back in a few days."

She nodded, her eyes welling with tears again. She stuck out her first two fingers on each hand and moved her fists together in a circular motion. She was telling me something in sign language. I felt horrible for not having studied that book harder.

Triven came to my rescue, squatting down beside us. "We will, you be careful too. Listen to Veyron, okay?"

"And don't let Maribel get you into any trouble." I added, thinking of her boisterous friend.

Mouse threw her arms around my neck and squeezed tightly. I clutched her in return, my tiny lifeline. I swallowed hard as she hugged Triven and took Veyron's hand.

"Take care of her." I didn't mean for it to sound like a threat, but it did. Okay, maybe I meant it just a little.

Mouse's brave face tore at me more than her tears. She was strong, like me, but I hated it. She should be playing happily with her friends, not worrying that two people she loved might die. I turned and headed for the door before her tears could trigger my own.

The night air felt stale when we reached the rooftop. I turned my face toward the grey-green sky, willing it to wash away all of the worry and guilt weighing me down. If I wanted to survive the next four days I needed a clear mind. I could feel Triven close behind me, careful as always not to touch me unless I initiated it. I wanted to lean back to feel his chest pressed to my back, warm and sturdy, but I didn't. *Clear head* I reminded myself.

"Where are we going first?" Triven asked.

"To see The Master." I turned to face him. "I need you to keep up with me. It's imperative you don't ask questions and don't fall behind. When we get there... he is a little... unorthodox. He will try to kill us, especially you. He is not kind to those he doesn't know. Protect yourself, I can handle my own. Whatever you do, don't kill him."

If Triven was worried he didn't show it.

I turned my back on him and gave him one last warning. "Don't let him kill you either."

I never had to look back to see if Triven was following me or not. His feet were as silent as mine, but I could feel him. Our other counterparts had done their jobs. Unlike most nights, the city wasn't quiet. Pillars of swirling smoke rose in various sectors and random gunfire could be heard echoing through the streets. Tartarus was at war again and this time it was our hands that fired first. The Subversive was still unseen, but we were no longer hiding.

My feet slowed as we reached The Master's hideout. He had taken over a huge old building that had some kind of vault in its basement. I had seen it once when I was younger. The door was nearly a foot thick with three-inch thick bars that protruded out of it when engaged by a wheel on the front. Mostly I remember the sound— it was so final when that door shut. Like it would never open again. This was the room I hoped to see today. Inside was a collection of weapons and gadgets that could rival the Ravagers. I was pretty sure there was also something more valuable there. Maps. Maps of the city before The Devastation, which were supposedly lost. As well as maps of The Sanctuary, which were worth more than my weight in weapons. I vaguely remembered them on the wall, hidden behind plated glass. I only hoped my memory was not playing tricks on me.

I could see his building three roofs ahead of ours. Surely he knew of our presence already. Now it was just waiting for him to make the first move. I felt the ground beneath us shake as something exploded a few miles away, a new plume of smoke rising. Triven hesitated behind me. I hissed though my teeth to keep him moving.

My ears registered the sound before my other senses could. I dropped and kicked Triven's feet out from beneath him. The knife barely nicked his left ear as he went down. No sooner had his back hit the ground, he was rolling onto his feet again. Three more knives pierced the night, one narrowly missing my head and two others imbedding themselves into my backpack as I twisted away. I dropped the bag— its weight making me feel unbalanced— as my hands moved to my weapons.

I barely had my knife out of its holster before his first blow landed. Something reminiscent of a foot struck my chest forcing the air from me. My body recoiled backwards as my feet flipped upwards. Tucking with the momentum, I rolled back over my shoulder into a crouch. I could hear more collisions of flesh, like meat hitting meat. Triven was now engaging him. A body flew past mine, grunting as it hit the tar, and I sprang back into the fight.

I had forgotten how fast The Master moved. How hard it was to follow, to predict him, but I held my ground. Blood was trickling down my nose, the coppery taste catching on my lips. There was an opening as his left hand moved for another knife. With a quick thrust I smashed my fist into his exposed nose. It crunched beneath my hand. As I drew back something hard collided with the side of my head causing my left eye to go black. When I blinked again my face was against the rooftop. Feet were dancing in and out of my sightline and it took me a minute to remember who they belonged to. I forced my feet back into submission underneath me and rose unsteadily.

Triven was on the ground now, a taller and leaner man sitting astride his half conscious body. The knife pressed into his throat was trailing a thin line of blood as The Master pushed against Triven's restraining hands. Triven was managing to keep the blade from sinking in deeper, but just barely.

I pressed my gun to the back of The Master's unruly, shaggy dark head. "I wouldn't do that if I were you."

"No fair bringing a gun to a knife fight." His strange accent was still thick even after all these years.

"Weren't you the one who taught me only a fool brings just knives." I kept the barrel pressed to his skull, my finger on the trigger.

He laughed as he retracted the blade from Triven's throat. "Glad to see something got into that thick skull of yours."

He rose to his feet, his dark eyes studying me as he stepped back from Triven's body.

Keeping my gun on him, I reached out to help pull Triven to his feet.

"Weapons." I nodded at the ground.

With a rye smile the tall man began to unload an

impressive amount of weaponry from his body. Once the metallic clanking stopped and his pockets appeared empty he began to walk away. I nodded at Triven to pick up a few of the knives, and with my gun still aimed between his shoulder blades, we followed The Master to his lair.

16. ALLY

We shadowed The Master over the next two rooftops. I had never accessed his building the same way twice. Every time I had entered through an access, it would be thoroughly sealed off by my next visit. Our encounter with The Master had not been as bad as I had expected— a few bumps and bruises, maybe a broken finger. The first time I met him he knocked me out cold for the better part of the day. He said the only reason he didn't kill me was because I was a kid and I could be good trading leverage to a Tribe. When I offered him a long-term agreement of exchanging food, weapons and books for his training he knocked me out again while he thought about it. Apparently my first two lessons were how to take a hit. I was twelve.

We went in through an abandoned elevator shaft this time. The Master jumped carelessly into the shaft, zipping downward at an alarming speed. He didn't care if we followed or not. If we were too scared, he wouldn't have to deal with us. If we fell to our deaths, no one would ever have to deal with us again.

I made sure Triven watched closely as I wound my legs around the cables and gripped tightly with both hands. His eyes flickered for just a moment as I slid down the shaft into the darkness. I could feel him climb on above me as the cables whizzed beneath the soles of my boots. It seemed to take forever, the friction beginning to burn even my callused hands. I feared a body would come rushing past me, that Triven would lose his grip. But he held on. The Master waited until both our feet met the bottom of the shaft, then he moved onward. We moved silently in the dark. It had only been minutes, but it felt much longer, the darkness devouring the time. I jumped when light filled the hallway. Repressing the urge to shield my eyes, I followed The Master's outline through the door.

Everything was as I remembered it. There were no windows, only concrete walls adorned with elaborate pillars. There was still a makeshift mat in the center where he had taught me to fight. Old bloodstains still soiled the surface, some of them undoubtedly mine. The polished stone floors were littered with junk. Boxes were stacked here and there, along with random books and bundled paper. Tiny bands grouped the stacks of paper with numbers on them, each group imprinted with a man's face I didn't recognize. Whatever they once were, The Master now used them as kindling. I watched as he tossed two bundles into his dying fire. In the light I could see him better. He had aged since I last traded with him. It had been nearly two years. His dark hair was now peppered with grey. As always he was a handsome man, with honey skin and full lips. His almond-shaped eyes were bright and intrusive as he watched us enter. I stopped just inside the room, Triven stopping with me.

I broke the silence. "Triven this is The—"

"Xavier." Triven cut me off. My eyes jumped to his face. Anger was apparent in his clenched jaw, but only to me.

"I haven't heard that name in quite some time boy. And how did you come by it may I ask." I could see The Master's hand move to the knife I knew was hidden at his hip.

"I recognize your face from my mother's photo." Triven sat back against a table, keeping his calm façade. "It's

142

not every day one meets another deserter from The Sanctuary."

My head whipped back so fast my neck kinked. "You're from The Sanctuary?!"

"Aye child. You didn't think your father came upon my name by luck now did you?"

"But you never told me." I almost shouted, clenching my fists.

"You never asked." He shrugged, his hands relaxing a little. Turning back to Triven, he continued. "You must be Vox and Arstid's child. I can see the resemblance to your father. How are two of my favorite rebels? "

"My father died shortly after coming here and I am sure my mother would be pleased to know you have been hiding here the whole time."

Xavier pressed his fingers to his lips, "I am sorry to hear about your father, he was a good man."

Triven nodded in acceptance, his deep eyes trained on the floor. I would have to ask for an explanation later.

"What brings you here Phoenix? Your skills could obviously use refining, but I get the feeling that's not why you're here."

I mentally cringed at his rebuke. "We are here for information."

"Information doesn't come cheap these days girl." He tossed another green bundle of paper onto the fire as he eyed us.

I placed my bag on the table between us and pulled out the knives and the heat-seeking gun. The bomb I left tucked away. No point giving away all of our leverage. Triven showed no sign of surprise as I laid out the weapons. I wondered if he knew I had them the whole time or if he just was better at hiding his feelings than I thought. I stepped away from the table to let The Master— or Xavier or whatever the hell his name was— inspect my offerings.

His expression was not so convincing. There was a spark in his eyes as he ran his hands over the weapons in turn, lifting the gun and flipping the knives in his hands. Every time his hands moved I could feel Triven tense behind me. But I wasn't worried. If he had wanted us dead we would be already.

"You found the way in?" His eyebrows rose in disbelief.

I shook my head. "That is why we are here to see you."

"The only way I know into The Sanctuary was sealed off long ago. I cannot help you." He stepped back from the weapons, still gazing longingly at them.

"There were maps you used to have." His fierce glare told me I had hit a nerve, I wasn't supposed to remember that.

"Those maps are not for trade." He narrowed his eyes. "Besides what could two children like you want with them?"

I snarled at his use of the word children. Triven spoke before I could lash out.

"The Subversive is rising. We plan to overthrow The Minister and take back what is ours."

Or just escape Tartarus. I thought to myself.

"I would love to see The Minister fall…" Xavier pondered. "His misery would bring me great joy. But these measly weapons you offer are not worth my maps."

I reached inside my bag and pulled out the silver coated bomb, letting my fingers trace over its flawless surface. His eyes lit as they watched my fingers.

"We may be able to strike a deal after all."

Fifteen minutes later, the maps were safely folded into my backpack and we were back outside on top of Xavier's building. I was ready to leap to the next rooftop, anxious to get to a safe house and examine the maps in greater detail, but Triven had paused.

"If we move on the city, will you join us?" He asked Xavier.

The man I had known as The Master clapped a large hand over Triven's shoulder and shook his head.

"I have no desire to kill one ruler just to be forced under the thumb of another. I am the only ruler I need. The maps are dated and won't tell you everything, but they are a start. If my sources are correct— and they usually are— you need to seek out the Ravagers' meeting place, a building in the upper west quadrant. All I ask is that you remember my trade with you was fair and leave me to myself when the time comes." He turned to me. "You're still one of the best naturals I have met, but don't get sloppy. If you need refining, you know where to find me."

I nodded respectfully and we set out across the rooftops once more.

On any normal night, I would have rolled my dice and headed for a random safe house, but tonight was different. Other Subversive guards now occupied several of my safe houses and our goal was to place ourselves near the next target, which didn't leave us many options. To narrow it down further, there were some places I could barely fit into, and there was no way Triven's larger frame could maneuver the cramped access routes. We passed through the night unseen, but I was on edge. I had to remind myself that this is how I had lived for so many years, a shadow on the rooftops, that it was normal. The only difference was I had never done it with someone else. As we ran I narrowed our options down to two places, the old transport station or the clock tower. Last time I had stayed at the transport station several Scavengers were sniffing around for scraps. I loathed their vile stink. Even the thought of them triggered my gag reflex.

The clock tower it was.

At an earlier time, the jump to the dilapidated tower would have been impossible. But during some point of the world's decay a nearby building had fallen into its side, giving someone with nimble feet, like me, the perfect approach. While I moved lithely over the crumbled stones, I could hear Triven's progression slow down. I waited a little impatiently for him before leaping up to the next ledge and pulling myself over. He landed next to me panting.

"You're lucky you're so small. I was worried that rubble

wouldn't hold my weight." He pressed his hands to his knees.

"Almost there. Come on, we can rest once we're inside." I chided him.

The tower was just as I had left it. It was a large room with four round glass windows on each wall. They were three times my height and frosted an aged white. I am sure at some point they were beautiful and illuminated but now they were merely stained with dirt and decay. A few roman numerals still clung to the outside faces, while rusted gears protruded inwards. You could just make out the clock hands on the other side. We couldn't light a torch in here for fear of being seen, but the room just up the spiral staircase was invisible to the outside.

"Home sweet home." I murmured as we entered the windowless maintenance room and lit the torch.

"How often did you live here?" Triven asked as he ran his fingers over the food preserves I had stashed on a shelf.

"Only sometimes. It's merely one of my safe houses. You know, a different one every night." I shrugged, feeling self-conscious. But his eyes were warm and admiring as they fell on me.

"This is amazing. You're amazing."

I flushed and began rifling through my bag for another torch. "Anyone would have done this. It's just about surviving, that's all."

When I rose, his chest was right in front of me. I looked up at him as his hand reached for my face, but he stopped just before touching me.

"No Prea, most people would have just given up and let the city consume them. You, however, have made this city yours. You bent it to your will and took control of your own destiny. You are amazing."

I pressed my face to his palm, closing the gap between us. The instant my skin touched his, his lips found mine. And for the first time in my life I let myself forget that I was in the city of Tartarus.

***

When I awoke there was light seeping in from under the closed door. I mentally kicked myself for not sealing it off properly last night. On my own, I would have never made a mistake like that.

Triven's arms were draped around me, his breath tickling my ear. I blinked at the unfamiliar daylight streaming in. This was the second time my nightmares had not plagued me. At first I thought maybe it had been whatever was in Cook's hooch, but this time the only common factor was Triven.

We had spent the night in a feverish embrace, our lips never getting enough, but our romantic exploits stopped there. Not that we didn't want more— we did— this just wasn't the time or the place. And if I was being honest with myself, I wasn't ready and somehow he knew that. I wasn't sure I could let myself connect to another person that intimately. Sharing myself like that meant giving a piece of myself away, and right now I was barely holding onto the pieces I had left.

I pulled away from Triven, pausing as he mumbled in his sleep. Quietly, I grabbed the maps and headed back down to the clock room. A greenish light poured in from all of the opaque faces. I paused, drinking in the light. This was the closest I had come to seeing daylight in almost six years. I knew the sun of Tartarus was not the one of my childhood. Out here the atmosphere was tainted by decay. If I went outside, there would be no blue sky, or golden sun. Just haze and smog that tinged the sun's rays a greenish brown. It was easier to stand behind the frosted glass clock faces and pretend the world outside was that of my childhood rather than to face the truth of my reality.

After spreading the two maps over the aged floor, I folded my knees beneath me and began to study the pressed pages. The Master had kept them in perfect condition, the delicate papers only tinged slightly with inevitable age. Even

147

after all of the years I had stood on rooftops looking down on the city, it still seemed strange to see it from this view, from so high above. One map contained elaborate photographs of the city before it crumbled into Tartarus. Vehicles could be seen on the streets, people on the sidewalks, no protruding mountains or wastelands to be seen. The aerial projection seemed surreal. The buildings stood straight, the streets were whole, it seemed nothing like the city I knew. But hidden in the structured order was something familiar. Shapes, that while whole, triggered some kind of recognition.

The other map was hand-drawn in great detail. There was no mistaking the dense line that represented The Wall. Outside of the line was nothing, like the world there didn't exist. Inside there were marked buildings. The Master had labeled the structures from his memory but to me the sketched buildings meant nothing. I was actually disappointed I couldn't remember. Overlapping the two maps I joined the two worlds. The Wall seemed so much larger looking at it like this, so... impenetrable. That dark line was the only barricade between my past and my future. I traced the line. There were no tunnels, no hidden gaps in the heavy ink.

I pressed two fingers to my forehead and closed my eyes as I tried to visualize the maps in my mind.

I was sitting on top of the clock tower looking at the city below me, the city I knew. The buildings rose from the map in my mind like a popup book. The rubble and decay pressed against the impenetrable Wall. I could see it all. Placing my fingers on the map I traced the buildings as I visualized them. A creak on the stairs told me Triven was awake.

He was watching me, for how long before the old stairs gave him away I wasn't sure. My fingers stopped as I met his eyes. The look in them brought a flush to my cheeks. He was wearing only an old grey stained tank top and his linen pants, his long-sleeved shirt removed sometime in his sleep. His bare skin was dark in the late daylight, the scars from years of surviving the streets prevalent against the otherwise smooth surface. His muscles flexed as he moved down the stairs towards me. A thin line of dried blood still clung to his neck where The Master had cut him last night. The warmth of his eyes was magnified in the strangely green fading light. He looked like a warrior, like a god. I pushed away the feelings stirring in my chest. He loved me. I could see it in his eyes. But did I feel the same way? It was easier to be angry, to be alone. Love was scary. It was opening myself up to possible pain. But as he folded himself next to me to examine the maps, I knew I wanted him here. I needed him here. But did that mean I loved him? Or was I just being selfish, wanting his love but not willing to give mine in return?

"Is it my imagination or does it seem like a lot of the Ravagers' warehouses border The Wall?" Triven's finger traced the same line mine had.

I glanced back down at the maps, thankful for the distraction. He was right. Even now where my finger lay frozen, it fell over the Ravagers' food warehouse. In fact, six of their well-known hangouts fell along The Wall. I pulled my hand back as his came too close. He didn't seem to notice. I watched as his fingers moved to the map of The Sanctuary.

"What was it like there?" My words were barely audible. I didn't look up, but I could feel Triven's eyes on me. It took him a minute to answer.

"I wasn't much older than you when we left The Sanctuary. There are things that I remember clearly and other things that are hard to separate from the stories my mother has retold me over the years. There were good things though. I remember having friends, going to classes and learning. I remember blue skies and sunshine. We never went hungry or worried about shelter. Every person was provided food and a home to live in and in return every citizen contributed to society. It was supposed to be a utopia." I looked up to find him smiling sadly as he stared at the map, but it faded quickly.

"But that was just a façade. Life there was…measured. Everything we did, from when we ate to what we wore to what jobs we could work, was controlled. There were rules that had to be adhered to and those few who did not, tended to disappear. We were controlled by fear. I remember a boy in one of my classes questioning Minister Fandrin's leadership during a history lesson. The teacher lashed him in front of the class, saying the boy's impertinence should be a lesson for us all. He said the student was lucky he was only a child or he would have been thrown out into Tartarus for treason."

I felt my chest tighten as Triven's eyes met mine. Something in his words resonated in my broken mind.

"Military personnel dominated our population. There isn't a day I can remember where they weren't present in our lives. Walking the streets, arresting miscreants, enforcing the peace." He shook his head pensively. "That's quite the oxymoron isn't it? *Enforcing* peace. As a child I thought the military was there to keep us safe, to protect us from the monsters that were outside of The Wall. But now, I realize it was never about protecting us, it was about controlling us." Triven sat back from the maps, chewing absently on his thumbnail as he got lost in his own memories.

My mind was whirling with information. I wished I could remember something, anything, that somewhere in my brain Triven's words would trigger some of my lost memories, but there was nothing. My past was still just a void. My fingers unconsciously traced the scar hidden beneath my hair. To my surprise Triven's fingers followed mine, his hand cupping my face as they traced over my scar.

"Do you think this is why you can't remember?" Concern flared in his gentle features.

I shrugged, shaking my head as I pushed his hand away.

"It's going to be dark soon, we should eat and get ready to leave. The building The Mas-Xavier told us about is not far from here. I would like to scope it out tonight. If we have to be out in the daylight to follow their movements I want to plan our hiding places. It's better if we stack the odds in our favor." I got up and stretched. "I'll find us something to eat. See if you can get anything else from the maps."

***

Two hours later we were in motion again. As a precaution I packed up all of our things. Triven wanted to spend another night in the clock tower, but every particle of my being told me to move on. Too many years on the run had perhaps skewed my judgment on safety, but then again, it had also kept me alive.

The building was less than a mile from our hiding place and we made good time. Only once did we have to hide in the shadows as a group of Wraiths passed below us. I could hear the rattling of the human bones they wore around their necks as grotesque trophies before we saw them. Based on their formation, they were hunting someone. I hoped it was not one of our own. When they passed we moved on.

I knew the building Xavier spoke of. It was in the middle of an old warehouse district by the decaying canal. The entire area reeked of sewage. Eventually we had to pause to drape cloths over our noses and mouths as the smell became too overpowering. To most people the building looked just like the other dilapidated buildings in the area, but to me it was clearly a hideout. Unlike the surrounding buildings, all the windows and doors had been sealed off. They were blocked with graffitied boards, fallen rubble, or wrought iron bars. What looked like clusters of trash were actually well-placed barricades. After two laps around the building we realized the only way in were the double doors at the back of the alley. We were going to have to enter on street level. This meant exposure.

I hated exposure.

Leaving our bags concealed in an air duct and heavily laden with weapons, we began to climb down toward the streets. As our feet touched the pavement, a pack of wild dogs howled in the distance. A shiver of fear ran down my spine and we hastened our steps. The door was hidden in the shadows, barely visible from ground level. Sliding behind the dumpster, Triven followed my lead. There were no bolts on the doors, no chains to keep the unwanted out. Only the Ravagers would be so intentionally careless.

Mirroring my movements, Triven pressed his ear to the door. Our eyes locked as we listened for something, anything. His hazel eyes were clear windows to his thoughts. Despite his calm pretense, worry and fear still swam in their depths. I wondered if he saw the same in my own. We waited nearly a minute, unmoving and barely breathing, but no sounds came from inside.

With a hesitant nod, I moved to open the doors. But as my hand reached for the handles, Triven's fingers wrapped around my wrist holding me back. I snapped to his face to question him, but my words caught in my throat. His worried eyes had steeled. He firmly shook his head and pulled me behind him. I knew what he was saying. This wasn't about being chivalrous or his pride. He was telling me I was more important, that my life was worth more than his. Pain rose in my chest as he pulled back the door and entered first.

He had it wrong. He was the good one, the better of the two of us. I was too damaged, but Triven still had hope. Anger rose within me. How dare he choose me over himself. You had to look out for number one first if you wanted to survive here. And I needed him alive. Mouse needed someone better than me. She needed him. She deserved him.

As Triven moved into the shadows beyond the door, I pulled my gun and turned, scanning the alley again. If he was going to insist on playing the fool then the least I could do was watch his back. I backed through the doorway behind him keeping my eyes alert for any movement. I shifted with Triven in a backwards dance. As he moved to close the door, I scanned the vast darkness in the warehouse. When the door closed behind me, it took everything I had not to scream. I swallowed back the rising panic. Despite my restraint, I jumped back into Triven's chest when a light came on. It wasn't bright but it was enough to see. My eyes flew around the room looking not for the source but for who turned it on.

"It's triggered by the doors." Triven whispered. I turned as he thumbed a latch by the door causing the lights to flicker. "When the door opens the lights go out."

"That seems unusually smart for a Ravager." I muttered stepping further inside and pulling the cloth from my mouth. The stench from outside hadn't penetrated the walls.

We were unquestionably alone. The huge room was barren, stripped down to the shell and structure. The floors were solid concrete with a few drainage grates. Conspicuous rust colored spatters flecked the grey surface. The walls were made of smooth cinderblock and the ceiling was nearly forty feet up. Even I would have a hard time getting up to the few exposed beams above us. There was no furniture, no racking and no chance of concealment.

Triven's forehead was pinched as he made the same assessment. There was no place to hide and only one way out. This place was a death trap and we both knew it. Raising our guns, we both began to move back towards the door.

We were less than ten feet from the door when my skin began to crawl. Triven stiffened by my side.

We had both heard it.

The distinct sound of gravel crunching beneath shoes. As the foot falls got louder there were muffled voices that accompanied them. The hair rose on the back of my neck. I could hear the clinking of metal piercings, the squeal of leather rubbing on leather. Fear and adrenaline began to pulse through my veins. They were Ravagers. But the part that worried me was that they were speaking in hushed tones. Never in my life had I ever heard a Ravager advance quietly.

They would open that door in mere seconds and we were trapped.

17. DECEIT

My eyes naturally took to the ceiling, searching the beams for a place to hide even though I knew there was nothing there. Everything was too open, too exposed. The rapid beating of my heart pulsed in my ears. We were trapped. I jumped when Triven's hand closed around my wrist.

I turned to meet his green eyes. Instead of finding panic, they were strangely apologetic. "I'm sorry, but it's the only way. I will be right here with you."

My eyes traveled to his left hand. It was holding up a metal grate in the floor. The tendons in my throat constricted violently. Before I could pull away, he yanked forward, throwing me effortless under the grate. It was all I could do not to scream. I fell face first into the shallow pit, the stench instantly transforming me back into that scared eleven-year-old. I pushed myself up, trying to escape, but Triven's body crashed down on me pinning me to the ground. He pushed me onto my back and laid down next to me as the grate clanked shut. The bars seemed to close in, pressing in on me, crushing me. My body began to shake uncontrollably.

"Close your eyes." Triven whispered. There was fear in his voice, but it was still steady. "I'm here, Prea. I'm not leaving you."

I pressed my palm over my mouth, stifling my ragged breathing just as the door opened. The light went out as they moved inside. Shadows passed over us and I stopped breathing. Then the door clicked shut and the light came back on. The sole of a dress shoe was hovering inches from my face. I closed my eyes. Our hiding place was cast into shadow. The dim light was barely strong enough to reach us and with our dark clothing we would just disappear. As long as they didn't look down for too long we just might remain unseen.

I tried to envision myself somewhere else, anywhere else, but the smell was too familiar. Closing my eyes only made it worse, but I couldn't make them open. I could see my parents' faces, their blood spilling onto the darkened pavement. My mother's screams began to echo in my ears.

Triven's hand closed over mine, squeezing lightly, pulling me back from the darkest depths of my mind.

I tried to calm myself.

I wasn't alone. We were together.

I tried to focus on the voices talking above us.

"Please tell me you're not wasting my time with this drivel. Have you found what I asked for?" A deep voice silenced all of the others.

"We did—"

I recognized the second voice, but couldn't place it.

"Then why are you empty-handed?" The deeper voice was like ice. It trickled down my eardrums chilling its way to my bones.

"There was a complication..."

"I don't have time for complications. We have paid you handsomely and expected results."

"We know, we are—"

"I don't think you do. I think you have forgotten who's in charge."

I bit into my palm as the gunshot rang out. There was a hollow thud of a body hitting the concrete floor. Even with my eyes closed I knew it was blood that splattered my face. The warm droplets dripped down my cheek, pooling as they caught in the hollow of my ear. The salty copper smell made my stomach churn. I pressed my fingers over my nose to keep from breathing, trying to suppress the gag spasming in my throat. It was too much. The smell of the blood mixed with the stench of the sewer. Images of my parents' deaths were flashing in my mind again. I barely heard the man speak above us.

"Next time it will be *your* head. Find the girl."

The noises swirled around me. More voices, sounds of feet and something heavy being dragged away. It was dark and then light again. Then there was silence, dragging, agonizing silence.

As soon as Triven lifted the gate I exploded past him, barely making it to my knees before I retched. My body was heaving and shaking so violently my teeth rattled. Something touched me and I lunged to my feet, backing away.

Triven reached for me again and I bolted. I didn't remember touching the door or scaling the wall we had so carefully climbed before, but I was on the rooftops again somehow. Something warm wetted my cheeks and my eyes began to blur, but I still ran. I ran until I couldn't feel my legs, until I couldn't breathe.

I collapsed, the rough rooftop cutting into my knees and palms. A high-pitched keening reverberated from my chest. I knew I should be quiet, that I should stop, but I couldn't. Someone was approaching me, but I didn't care. Let them kill me. Let them stop my pain. But there was no such luck.

I didn't cringe when he touched me this time. Instead I fell back into his waiting arms. They were so warm, so desirable. At that moment I wanted to feel something, anything other than the building pain. I wanted to forget. Forget my past. Forget my name.

Triven stiffened as I crushed my lips to his. He hesitated.

"Please." I pleaded between kisses. "Please... I need to

feel something, anything other than this. Please…"

I let out a sigh of relief as his lips responded to mine. They were hesitant but he was giving in. But it wasn't enough. The tears were still streaming down my face, salting our kisses. I needed more. I wanted to lose all of the pieces I had been hanging on to. I didn't want them anymore. I didn't want to be *me* anymore.

My hands roamed to his chest, pushing up his shirt, pulling at the buttons on his pants. His reaction was instantaneous. He pushed me away, grabbing my wrists to restrict my hands. His eyes were wide with pain and understanding.

"No Prea. Not like this."

I crumpled in defeat, letting my hands fall limp in his grip. Then the sobs came, wracking my body with fierce convulsions. Heavy arms wrapped around me, gathering me in their shelter. It hurt. Everything hurt. All of the pain I had repressed for so many years flooded my mind, drowning me. It could have been minutes or hours or days, I didn't know. I thought maybe I would die from the pain, but it only persevered. The only thing that held me to this earth, that kept my life grounded, were the arms holding me.

***

Eventually the sobs quieted and my body slowly stopped shaking. Triven kept me pressed to his chest, but he never said a word. I was revolted with myself. Despite all of my bravado, all my effort to keep up the hardened façade, he now knew how broken I was. And there was no taking it back. I hated him… I hated that he made me get into the grate. I hated that he was stronger than me. I hated that he was a better person than I was. But what I hated most is that I didn't hate him at all.

Honestly, it scared me. For years I had repressed my emotions, choked back my fear just as I did my screams every morning. But tonight, in that grate, everything finally caught up to me. Despite my best efforts I couldn't outrun my past. The repressed memories mauled me with their razored talons until I lay raw and naked. The little girl I had thought died—that I had desperately wanted to die in the alley— was still alive somewhere in me. And her presence burned. The little girl had never left. I had just bound and gagged her. Kept her temporarily silent.

Then, something in my mind clicked. Words came to me through the haze. What had the deep-voiced man said tonight?

"Find the girl." I whispered to myself as the gears clicked back into place. A completely different kind of fear overshadowed my thoughts.

"What?" Triven relaxed his grip on me. Pushing him away I sprung to me feet in a panic.

"Find the girl!" I screamed at him.

He looked back at me lost. His dark eyebrows pulled together.

"Find *the* girl, Triven! Those men tonight, they were from The Sanctuary weren't they?" My body was vibrating with tension.

"Yes... well some of them I think. But there were Ravagers too, the one with the eye patch seemed to be in charge."

I was thankful he had kept his eyes open when I could not. I knew I recognized that voice.

"I know who they're looking for." I snatched my bag from Triven's side. He must have grabbed it before following me. I turned and started walking in the opposite direction, shoving all of my own pain back down.

"How?" Triven grabbed his bag and jogged after me, perplexed.

"Because of the man with the eye patch."

"You know him?"

"I'm the one who gave him that eye patch. I threw a

knife in his eye when I rescued the girl from him." I stopped dead, staring pointedly at him.

"It's Mouse…" He realized his eyes widened with fear.

18. MOUSE

I knew that Mouse was safe right now, that the Ravagers would never find her while she was hidden within The Subversive. But even so, I could not make the roofs move fast enough beneath my feet. The sallow sun was just spreading its first rays when we finally reached the hidden doors.

The guards were surprised by our sudden appearance. While Triven paused to explain the situation I plowed on ahead. I didn't have time for silly questions. I needed to see Mouse, hold her tiny hands. I needed to know she was okay. I pushed through the people in the halls, barely seeing them. It was early morning. Mouse should be in the dining hall or possibly with Maribel. After I nearly knocked down a frightened looking youth, Triven finally caught up to me. For the first time I could remember, he grabbed my arm, pulling me to a halt. He flinched when I turned on him and I tried to soften my gaze.

"You should shower first." He held tight to my upper arm as I tried to yank it away.

"Don't tell me what I need, Triven." I seethed. "What I *need* is to see Mouse. Right now."

"I know." Triven said. "She is eating with Maribel and

Veyron right now. I asked the guards."

I gritted my teeth. Why hadn't I done that?

"She is safe. But if you storm in there right now you will frighten her along with everyone else in that room."

As if on cue a woman passed us. She recoiled as she glanced at me, the color draining from her face. I really looked at Triven for the first time since the warehouse. He was covered in black filth. Streaks of blood were spattered across his clothing and face. It was hard to tell if it was his or not, like he maybe had murdered someone. I rubbed my free hand against my own face and it too came away bloody.

"Fine." He let go this time when I jerked away. I knew my anger at him was misdirected, but I didn't care. It was easier not to care. Caring meant pain. My little outburst tonight had proven that. I knew I couldn't shut him out forever, but at least for the next twenty minutes I could pretend.

My resentment lessened when I caught my reflection in the mirror. Of course he had been right. My stomach churned as I looked at myself. If Triven had looked frightening then I looked downright horrifying. I was filthy from our escapades in the city. Soot and grime were smeared over my pale skin, but more shocking was the spray of blood that covered my face like morbid war paint. Dried blood streaked my blond hair a grotesque russet, adorned by chunks of something I didn't want to think about. Had my stomach not been emptied already I would have been sick. I grabbed the shower handle, twisting it so the cold spray hit my face. I hadn't even taken off my clothes.

When I closed my eyes I saw blood. It was covering my face, seeping from my father's throat, my mother's chest. It was everywhere. I rubbed at my face, trying to wash it from behind my eyelids too. Finally I just opened them and stared at the water until it ran clean. It took forever. Slowly, I peeled off my clothing and began to scrub the blood from my pale skin. After getting dressed I gazed into the mirror looking for answers. The girl looking back at me was worn beyond her age, her blue eyes hard and cold, the rims red and swollen. She was a broken girl, a murderer, a product of this city. As I stared at her I knew the truth. As long as we were in Tartarus there would always be blood. If not my parents' or mine then it would be someone else's. It would never stop. Whatever childish dreams I had had about escaping into The Sanctuary, disappearing into their world, had vanished tonight. It wasn't about our world and theirs anymore. As soon as that man spoke tonight, as soon as his voice struck my ears, I realized the truth. Arstid had been right. There never was any them or us, we were one in the same. United in this forsaken hellhole. They were just the men behind the curtain, cruel and corrupt just like us. The blood would never stop flowing as long as The Wall kept us contained. We had to get into The Sanctuary and it had to be now. The Wall had to be breached. That barrier gave them power over us. They could come into our world whenever they saw fit, manipulating the Tribes to get what they wanted. I once thought The Wall was like a fence, meant to keep out the dangers of Tartarus. But the truth was, it was a cage meant to contain us. We were the ones trapped like rats, not the other way around. And if both sides were equally corrupt, breaching The Wall meant leveling the playing field. It was never about stopping the Tribes as I had thought. They were just the pawns. We needed to go after the leader. We needed to take down The Minister of The Sanctuary.

***

I found both Mouse and Triven in our room. Mouse leapt onto me as I entered, her tiny arms squeezing so hard it nearly hurt. My chest released a little— at least she was safe. I hesitantly met Triven's eyes, the shame for my behavior still fresh. But his eyes were as hard and admiring as ever. I was thankful for it. He had comforted me, held me while I fell apart. He had seen me at my worst and still there was no pity in his eyes, only strength. In that moment I understood. He didn't

162

pity me, he had never pitied me. Every hesitant touch, every gentle word wasn't because I was breakable, it was because I was a ticking time bomb, waiting to explode. No, he didn't pity me. He understood me.

Maybe better than I did myself.

Mouse flashed her hands at me when I finally pulled away. She was trying to ask me something, but I gathered her hands and shook my head to quiet her.

"Mouse, I have to ask you something, okay?" I knelt to her level.

Her wide eyes popped with trepidation, but she slowly nodded.

"You're from The Sanctuary aren't you?" Her brown eyes welled with tears. She shook her head violently, willing it not to be true. "Did I ever tell you I was from The Sanctuary? My mom and dad raised me there until I was about your age."

I choked a little as I mentioned my parents, but Mouse didn't seem to notice. Instead she shook her head slower, looking at me in a new light. I squeezed her hand as the tears broke loose and fell down her round cheeks.

"It's okay to be scared, but you're safe now. You're safe here with me…with us." I amended looking at Triven. "You escaped didn't you?"

She nodded hesitantly this time, unwilling to admit the truth.

"We escaped too. My family and I." I smiled encouragingly at her. I needed her to tell me the truth.

She signed to me again. *Mother. Father.* Then pointed at my chest with her eyebrows raised.

I struggled with the words. "They helped me escape, but they're not here anymore. They didn't… they're gone now."

Her face fell.

"Mouse, this part is very important. Do you remember how you got out?"

She stiffened, her tiny hands moving rigidly. *Why?*

163

"We need to get into The Sanctuary."

She began backing away, shaking her head again. Her hands shook as they signed. Her one hand was flat as she pulled the other fist with her thumb out over the top toward her chin repeatedly. I didn't know this one. My eyes turned to Triven for help.

"Danger. She's saying danger." Triven came to our level and gripped her frail shoulders. They were so small in his hands. "We know, Mouse. But it's not safe here either."

She looked apprehensively between us. And signed again. *No. Run.*

I took her hands in mine again.

"Mouse, I know you're scared. I'm scared too, all of the time. But I have been running for the last six years and I can't run anymore. Our world is falling apart. We aren't living, not really. We are just... surviving. I want you to have a better chance at a real life than I did. But to give you that, the world we know must be destroyed. From its ashes we will build new, but I need your help. We can't do this without you."

I could feel Triven's eyes on me as I spoke, but I kept my attention on Mouse.

Her eyes were still brimming with tears, but they brightened with determination now. She touched a palm to both Triven's face and mine. Then signed once more. Triven translated for me.

"Together."

19. INCEPTION

My little speech had worked. Mouse had gotten on board with our plans to infiltrate the walls. But it had worked too well. When she said "together" I assumed that it meant she would show us the way on the maps. Little did I know she meant to come with us. As I met his gaze from across the table, it was easy to see Triven was equally angry at me for not treating her more like a child.

Mouse had poured over the maps, her petite fingers tracing the city streets looking for something. There was understanding in her bright eyes, but when we asked her to show us the entrance she shook her head and signed. *Together.*

It clicked then for both of us. She didn't simply want to help us find the entrance, she wanted to come with us. No matter how hard we pressed her, she refused to relent. I even threatened to venture out on my own without her, but she knew the threat was useless. In one final attempt at intimidation, we set her before the council with the hope that she would buckle under the pressure. I hated the idea of sending such a small child to face a room of antagonistic adults— seeing as how even I found them intimidating— but the alternative was worse. If Mouse didn't tell us the location then we would have no choice but to bring her along. Just thinking about dragging her through the city where she couldn't defend herself made it harder to breathe.

Granted, I was not much older than her when I was left to fend for myself, but I had no other choice at the time. Mouse did. She didn't have to choose a life of bitterness and violence. She could still be a child and I didn't want to be the one to take that away from her. When I looked into her eyes I could see pain and fear from her past, but there was hope there too. That was something I never had and I would do everything in my power to ensure that spark of hope never faded.

To my frustration, however, a room of daunting adults didn't intimidate the child at all. Not even Arstid's sallow face held any power of coercion over Mouse. Part of me was proud. Most children would have been quelled by a room full of formidable adults, but not Mouse. She was stronger than she looked. I could see the determination in her frail features. She was not going to give in. As much as I wanted to keep her safe, to act as a parent to the small girl sitting beside me, I was not her parent. I was the person she had chosen to trust in this messed up world and watching her now, I finally realized it was time I trusted her.

"She should come with us." I said to no one in particular. My eyes were fixed on Mouse as she sat tall in her chair. Her head snapped towards me a grin spreading across her face.

"What?!" Veyron exploded from across the table.

"Phoenix." There was a warning in Triven's voice that cut at me.

There was an upheaval among the council members, but to my surprise there were several members who met my gaze in agreement. One set in particular was the last I would have expected.

"She's just a child!" Archer slammed her hand on the table, calling my attention.

166

"And how old were you when you went on your first hunting party?" I challenged her.

She glared at me, "That's not the same thing. I had no choice."

"You're right you didn't. Neither did I, but Mouse does. And she wants to do this. Don't misunderstand me, I am completely against exposing her to what lies ahead of us, but I also must respect her decision."

"Her decision?!" Veyron gestured at Mouse in disbelief. "She's a child, this isn't about *her* decision."

I met Mouse's hurt gaze. It was the first time I had truly seen her for who she was. Hidden underneath the innocence I could see her now, the little girl who had seen too much. She was not me, not so irreparably damaged, but she had been hurt. That much I knew. I spoke quietly, making those still speaking stop to hear me.

"She *is* young, but she is *not* a child anymore. I get that now. You all know better than most how this city can steal your innocence. Mouse may be young, but she has still suffered here just the same as the rest of us. We need her strength and knowledge, and in return she deserves our respect."

Mouse grabbed my hand, her round eyes full of gratitude. I could feel Triven's disapproval, but he said nothing.

"As much as it pains me to agree with Phoenix, she's right." All heads swiveled towards the severe voice. Arstid's hands were folded neatly on the table before her. "We're wasting precious time trying to extract information from this child. If she wants to risk her life, then that is her choice to make. We have laid in wait for nearly seven years and the time has come to take action. Supplies are beginning to run low and with the Tribe wars we have been initiating, this city has become a ticking time bomb. Right now we have the upper hand. Thanks to Triven,"— yeah, because it's not like I was there or anything— "we now know The Sanctuary has the Ravagers in their back pocket. Ultimately we are out-numbered and out-gunned. The only advantage we have is surprise. We

167

have managed to lay low for the better part of a decade, but that invisibility won't last for much longer. We need to strike now before we are discovered."

Even though several members still looked mutinous, no one spoke against her. Not even Triven. When no one disagreed, we began to formulate a plan.

***

It had taken us nearly four days of being trapped inside that unbearably stale room, but there was finally an agreed upon plan. There would be two armed parties. Triven and I would be heading team one. Mouse would be taking us to the passageway, and upon our safe entry, team two would escort her back to The Subversive bunker. Mouse was not pleased about this part of the mission. I knew she would put up a fight when the time came, but for now she played along. I knew this, because it was what I would do.

Our goal was to infiltrate The Wall and gather as much information about The Sanctuary as we could. The few remaining survivors from The Sanctuary had confirmed nearly everything on Xavier's map. I was surprised that one of them was Doc Porters. But a lot can change in six years. Buildings can fall and be rebuilt, people live and die, and power can change hands. When the defectors last left, they claimed The Sanctuary to be a place of repression, a false utopia. But, again, a lot could change in six years. Based on the weapons we had confiscated from the Ravagers, their weaponry had most certainly advanced. I hoped their politics had as well. As much as I yearned for a respite from the world I had come of age in, the hesitant fear I could see growing in Mouse's deep eyes made that hope dwindle.

Triven had not completely forgiven me for siding with Mouse. I didn't expect him to. He couldn't understand what it was like being alone in this world, what it was to carry a weight that was thrust upon you. There was a part of him that would never understand what Mouse and I saw in each other. Even though I could sense his doubts, he still stood firmly by my side. Part of me wished he would yell at me or push me away when I snuggled closer to him in my sleep, but he didn't. He was a better person than I was. I knew that, but still I could feel a tension growing between us that had not been there before.

Something had changed. When in his arms I had been able to sleep without the waking nightmares, but since that day when he forced me into the grate not even his arms could keep away the dreams. Something in my mind broke that day, cracked wide open and I couldn't close it. The nightmares had become worse. What was once a relentless echo of my parents' murders had morphed into a horrifying mix of echoes from the past and premonitions of the future. Instead of watching just my parents' deaths, I was now also forced to watch as Mouse and Triven were shot to death by a faceless man in a white suit. Somehow I knew he was from The Sanctuary, as if some forgotten memory from my childhood had filtered through the buried depths of my mind. I clawed relentlessly at the bars encasing me until my hands were raw, the blood dripping down my arms and face. Still the bars would not give. The screams I had trained myself to hold back could no longer be contained. I would wake in the middle of the night now, soaked in sweat, shaking as my screams filled our room.

Fortunately, Mouse had begun sleeping in the children's bunk now, because my fits would have terrified her. Despite our tension, Triven would gather me in his arms every night, holding me until I could regain control of myself again. Some nights it took longer than others for the shudders that rocked my body to dissipate. While Triven's presence always soothed me, I also despised him for it. I had always been so independent and strong and he had now seen me again and again at my weakest point. I told myself I didn't need him to quiet my screams or hold me until I stopped shaking, but I wanted him to. And I was angry with myself for that too. Being alone was easy, safe. Being with someone just complicated things.

We hadn't kissed since the night in the clock tower and I intended to keep it that way. Right now I needed my head clear. If my mind was cluttered with distracting emotions, I wouldn't be at the top of my game. And any hesitation or poor decision could cost me my life. Or worse, Mouse's or Triven's. My stomach clenched at the thought.

I watched Triven from across the weapons room as he suited up. His movements were strained, the muscles in his arms slightly flexed. Archer was testing her knives, repeatedly pulling them out of their holsters, feigning a throw only to replace them and repeat the process all over again. Arden was staring at something— or nothing— on the wall, his right knee bouncing at a rapid pace. There was an anxious buzz vibrating through the room. Even I adjusted my holster for what must have been the tenth time.

A brown head bobbed into my sightline, the round face was paler than usual. Mouse's eyes were wide. She flapped her arms in the too-long sleeves, looking slightly lost. I grabbed the front of her shirt and pulled her to me.

"Come here you." I smiled warmly at her and lowered my voice. "We are just being overly-cautious."

It was sort of true.

"Your part will be easy. You just have to promise to stay with me, okay? Then, once you show us the tunnel, you must listen to everything Veyron tells you. No excuses. While I'm gone she is going to look after you." I reminded her for what felt like the hundredth time.

Mouse nodded, trying to push up the long black sleeves that covered her fingertips. She looked so small. I carefully rolled up the ends so her hands could move freely. The shiny material felt scaly to the touch, the minuscule shields barely visible to the eye. Her body armor was not as good as the ones that were in the Ravagers' warehouse, but it was better than nothing. The thin materials could amazingly stop most bullets and protect against knives, but that didn't mean you couldn't be crushed or that a bullet couldn't cause internal damage from the impact. I could see the same shiny black material peeking out from beneath most of the guards' uniforms, but there wasn't enough for all of us. I had willingly given up mine to ensure Mouse would be safe. Even if it was too big on her, it could still save her life. If I was going into The Sanctuary for anything it was for her, for her future. And I needed to know that she would survive to live it, even if I didn't get to see it myself.

I could see the black material peeking out from Triven's collar. For once I was glad he listened to his mother's chiding. The new world we hoped for needed him. I was just a rogue, an outsider that relied too heavily on myself, who was too far removed. But Triven... he was the beacon his people needed. There were only four of the twelve of us who weren't wearing body armor, Arden, Maddox, Willets and myself. But only one other person knew I wasn't wearing mine. Triven, like the others, was under the impression that I was wearing body armor under my shirt. While lying to him about it left a foul taste in my mouth, it was the only way I could get him to agree to wear his own. I had clipped the bottom of the shirt I had given to Mouse and pulled the scrap around my collar to disguise my lack of armor. To anyone looking, it would appear my armor was peaking out from my shirt just the same as theirs.

Veyron's icy eyes met mine from across the room and we nodded to each other in understanding. I had pulled her aside one afternoon after fighting with Triven about who was wearing the armor. He had adamantly tried to force his on me, refusing to wear his if I didn't have one as well. I couldn't have that, I had already stacked the cards in Mouse's favor and I wasn't about to let his selflessness mess that up. To my surprise, Veyron didn't need much convincing. Like everyone else, she knew how special Triven was, that he was a leader they would soon need. I then preyed on her motherly nature to ensure Mouse's safety as well. In my mind there was no question that she would be wearing a suit. I needed someone else I could trust to survive as well. Besides, I had the best chance of surviving without help. It was what I was good at. It was what I had done for nearly seven years. But Mouse would need other people to survive, to care for her to protect her in case I failed. So I needed them to survive as well.

Veyron had always looked at Mouse with the same protectiveness I did and if anything happened to me, I knew she would take care of my young friend. After very little pressing Veyron agreed. She would wear the body armor perfectly concealed beneath her clothing, while I would fake wearing mine. To everyone else it would appear that she had graciously given her armor to me for Mouse's sake and then Triven no longer had an excuse not to wear his.

I ran my hands over my weapons again, going through my mental checklist. The people I wanted protected had the odds in their favor. I carried two long-range handguns and thirteen knives of various sizes hidden on my person. In a small pouch sewn into my jacket were my father's notebook and his pocket watch. In my backpack was a first aid kit from Doc Porters, two water canteens, the maps of the city, and a few MREs. Aside from the fact I had more weapons than I ever had before, I felt like myself again. The callous girl, who had braved the city for so long on her own, stirred within me.

People were starting to filter out of the weapons room. Dark should have fallen by now and the city would be waiting for us. I scanned the too quiet room again and noticed everyone had weapons except for Mouse. Making sure no one was watching us, I took a small knife from my boot and placed it in hers.

"Don't use this unless absolutely necessary. Don't try to protect anyone else. The only person you need to worry about is you. Do you understand?"

She nodded, her brown eyes serious.

If we failed we would all die, and in the depths of Mouse's eyes I could see her understanding of that. A chill

172

trickled down my spine. In minutes we would be letting a child lead us, following her towards two possible futures— surviving long enough to start a war or dying before the night was over.

20. DIVERTED

Our progression through the city seemed painfully slow compared to the nights I had run with Triven. There were many more of us this time and not every member of the guard was as agile or as fast as I would have liked. Mouse stayed at my side as I had instructed, only leaving it when we came to gaps between buildings that were too big for her to span. At these rare moments Triven would gather her in his arms and flawlessly make the leap with her held close to his chest. My heart stopped every time they jumped, only restarting when their feet were once again on solid ground.

It took us nearly an hour to reach the outskirts of the city. The massive base of the wall loomed high above the streets. As a reminder of its power, of our separation from their world, a bird slammed into the invisible shield towering above us. I could feel a collective jump from the group as the air crackled and the incinerated carcass fell to the streets. Only Mouse and I stood steady.

Gazing at the city below us, I mentally slapped myself. How many times had I stood on this exact rooftop? How many times had I passed right by the one thing I wanted most and never knew it was there? I should have known it would be here, of all places. It made the most sense.

I looked to Mouse for direction. "It's by the warehouse isn't it?"

She nodded, pointing to a dark shack of a building not ten feet from the Ravagers' food warehouse.

It all made sense now. The place I had first seen Mouse was not far from here and what better place to hide a passageway than one that is already guarded. I had always been so distracted by the food that I had never thought to look for more. Even now as we stood atop the skyline, three Ravager guards passed below on their rounds. No wonder those guards inside had always been so careless about their patrol of the food. It was never the food they were protecting.

Triven spoke first. "Team two will cover us from the rooftops. We will have to enter from street level. Veyron, take Mouse-"

Mouse tugged on his shirt interrupting him, shaking her head. She held out her hand and pressed her other index finger to it like a keypad.

Triven closed his eyes in exasperation. "There's a code isn't there?"

She nodded.

"And I'm guessing you're not going to tell us." I glowered at her, but she wasn't intimidated. Mouse signed *together* again then, folded her arms defiantly and shook her head. I wanted to hit something.

Triven opened his mouth to argue but I silenced him. "There's no time to waste arguing about it. Veyron, Arden and Willets will come with us. Once Mouse lets us in the tunnel you will get her back to safety. You two will cover us from above."

I pointed to Rowan and Baxter. I had seen what each of them was capable of with a gun. If they were acting as snipers from the rooftops, our chances were significantly better.

"Shoot anything that isn't us." Archer barked before they took off across the rooftops.

Triven's glare was cold when I finally met his eyes. I

knew he disagreed with me and if anything happened to Mouse he would never forgive me. In truth, I would never forgive myself either. He hoisted her up on his back and began to climb over the edge of the building into the dark alley below.

I brushed against Veyron and Willets as we moved toward the building's edge too. "I don't care if you have to knock her out or if she fights the whole way back. But once that door is opened, get Mouse the hell out of here."

I didn't wait for their response. Instead, I hurtled myself over the side of the building. My hands instinctively fell to the drainpipe I knew was there. Shoving off with my feet I twisted and caught the windowsill on the opposing building. In two more bounds I had passed Mouse and Triven and landed silently on the pavement with my gun drawn.

The streets were empty aside from the three guards outside of the warehouse and us. We were lucky they were lightly staffed tonight. I kept my eyes trained on the guards as I heard the feet falling in line behind me. After about a minute, I had counted all nine sets of boots as they reached the ground. There was a familiar sound of gun metal sliding from holsters. We were ready. I held my hand back; the tiny fingers I was reaching for were instantly in mine. I squeezed, reminding Mouse to stay with me. She squeezed back. We waited in the shadows for what felt like hours, but surely it was only minutes.

As soon as the guards began their loop, we slithered from our spot. It would be two minutes before they returned to the front of the building. I began counting off the seconds in my head. It only took fifty-four seconds to cross the open space. By sixty-three seconds we were all carefully hidden in the shadows of the buildings again. Mouse tried to pull ahead, but I tugged her back to my side. Triven nodded once at us. I could barely see the sheen of his eyes in the darkness. Keeping his gun raised, he moved in the direction of the building that looked more like a shack from this vantage point. My heartbeat pulsed in my ears as he disappeared through the warped doorway. The pulsing grew louder until he reappeared again.

He reached his hand out for Mouse. I pushed her into his waiting arms and spun back to the alley, keeping my eyes alert for any movement as I backed through the doorway after them. The room was tiny, hardly larger than the bunker we shared. I motioned for the others to wait; there was barely room for the three of us. Supports had fallen, dangling precariously from the ceiling and bricks lay in pieces on the floor. What might have once been wood floors, now looked more like dirt. I held my breath; fearful that if I moved too much the whole thing might collapse around us.

Mouse had moved into the corner of the room. Ducking under a huge fallen beam, she disappeared for a moment. I moved to follow her, but Triven's arm flung out stopping me.

Before I could push him away there was a series of mechanical tones and the brick wall beside us hissed open. My heart began to pound. It was here the whole time. A gust of stale air pushed against my skin.

Triven moved towards the opening but I stood frozen.

I was reminded that my parents had lost their lives to get me out and now I was intentionally going back in. A heavy sense of foreboding gripped me.

Something soft brushed against my arm and I snapped back to life. My fingers closed over her shoulders just as Mouse darted for the opening. She struggled, kicking with more power than I thought possible as I lifted her from the ground. I moved towards the door dragging her with me.

Willets moved into the doorframe just as we emerged, nodding once. "All clear. Make sure-"

Whatever he was going to say I would never know, for the moment I moved to hand over Mouse, his head snapped sideways as his blood sprayed my face. The life drained from his eyes as his body crumbled to the ground.

Screams erupted, dispersed with gunfire as chaos broke out around us.

I jerked back inside just as a bullet exploded the brick

next to my head. I could barely feel the tiny projectiles as they struck my face. Mouse had gone limp in my arms. At first, I feared she had been shot but her racing heartbeat told me it was merely fear. I twisted just as Triven's body collided with mine. I pushed Mouse into his arms and began shoving on his chest.

"Go! GO!" I screamed, pointing at the tunnel. Something flashed across his eyes before he turned and plummeted into the darkness.

There was more screaming from outside. I watched as the only two people I cared about disappeared and then turned to help those dying outside. I had only gotten a step outside the building before another bullet narrowly missed my head. I dove and rolled to my knees. The scene was full-blown pandemonium. Someone ran past me screaming something, but I couldn't hear him over the rain of bullets. His perfectly manicured blonde hair was streaked with blood. Bodies were strewn in the alley. There were ones clad in leather that I didn't recognize, but there was one trembling boy clutching his side that made my stomach lurch. Arden had been shot. His lips were terrifyingly white as he gasped for air. I jumped sideways firing at the rooftops as another bullet whizzed past my ear. Archer was engaged in hand-to-hand combat with a Ravager, while our snipers fired wildly at the roofs above us. Veyron was hunched over clutching her chest as she fired on the oncoming Tribesmen. While she was obviously in pain I could see no blood. I wordlessly said a prayer of thanks that I had insisted on her wearing the body armor. Maddox was smashing in the faces of anyone stupid enough to come within striking distance. I jumped to my feet and began firing rounds into the advancing crowd of Tribesmen.

We were outnumbered, but they were falling faster. Suddenly the fire from above ceased and when it began again it was the advancing Ravagers that began to fall. Rowan and Baxter had taken down the other snipers and were now protecting us from above.

Maybe we had a chance.

But even as the thought crossed my mind, a fire exploded in my right arm. I screamed, my body spasming as the bullet pierced my skin. The world tilted as I staggered sideways, the gun falling from my numb fingertips.

A new thought crossed my mind. If we couldn't fight, then I had to get them into the tunnel.

I lunged forward aiming for the injured Arden, but was knocked backwards by what felt like a brick wall.

Huge arms closed around me as I struggled to free myself.

"There's no time!" Maddox's gruff voice shouted into my ear.

I screamed something back at him. Most likely a string of profanities, but his grip was too strong for me. Plowing forward like a freight train he forced me back into the shack. His hand clamped painfully over my bullet wound and he threw me into the open passageway. My hands and face slammed to the dirt floor as I yelled in protest. I raised my head just in time to see his hulking outline as Maddox yanked the door shut behind us. The mechanical click of the bolts sounded like a death sentence.

21. GAME

At first I couldn't hear anything but shuffling feet and heavy breathing. As soon as the door closed all sounds of battle from the outside had died. Sitting in the musty tunnel, it was almost as if it had never happened.

But it did, I reminded myself.

Willets was dead, his blood still spattered on my face. And Arden didn't stand much of a chance either. None of them did for that matter. A torch's green light hummed to life somewhere further down the tunnel, casting its eerie glow.

"You left them to die." I said through gritted teeth. The adrenaline was wearing off. My bullet wound was beginning to throb.

Maddox was doubled over, leaning against the door he had just closed. His hands pressed against his knees as he raised his gaze to meet mine.

"What I did was save your life." His tone was bitter cold. "You're welcome."

He pushed off the door and walked past me further down the tunnel. Glaring at his back, I rose to my feet intent on punching him in the back of the head, but staggered. I sucked in a gasp of air as I moved too fast. Grabbing at my useless arm, I fell back against the tunnel wall.

"Phoenix?"

The light was coming closer, followed by Triven's voice. Mouse was carrying the lantern, but she stopped a few feet away staring at my arm. Triven however pushed around her, worry etching his face as he grew nearer. "You're bleeding."

I pushed myself upright and tried to move around him. "I'm fine really. It's just a scrape."

"She got shot." Maddox's voice carried out of the shadows ahead of us.

I opened my mouth to say something rather unpleasant in return but Triven distracted me. His hands were pulling not too gently at my arm and shirt, looking for the source of the blood.

"But you were wearing body armor, there's no way—" His words cut off as he yanked back the collar of my shirt revealing the scrap of fabric that hung uselessly around my neck. He then ripped my shirt, exposing my bleeding arm. His cheeks flushed red.

With a huge sigh, he pressed his forehead to mine. I stared up at him but he kept his eyes closed. When he spoke his voice was low and full of pain.

"Are you freaking kidding me? Do you have any idea how selfish, how *stupid* that was. I could have lost you."

I wished he had yelled at me. It would have been easier to deal with if he had been angry, but instead I realized just how badly I had hurt him. In my attempt to keep him safe I had caused him pain. Emotions always complicated things.

"I'm sorry."

It was the only thing I could think to say. I wasn't sorry that I had tricked him to keep him safe. I would do it again given the chance. But I was sorry I had hurt him.

He kissed me for the first time in over a week. It was rough and brief. And it made me long for more while feeling ashamed at the same time. Another green light came bobbing into view. It was the ponytailed blonde guard whose name I could never get right. Brant or Grant or something like that. He must have been the one who had rushed passed me outside. Coward.

"Where are the others?" He asked, glancing at the four of us. Maddox shook his head. "Oh. Well, the tunnel goes on for about another quarter mile. We should get moving."

"Are you okay to move?" Triven eyed my bleeding shoulder.

"I'm fine." I nodded.

Triven ripped off a strip of my tattered overshirt and pressed the fabric to my wound.

"Keep pressure on it." He murmured as he pressed his palm against the small of my back and began guiding me down the tunnel. Mouse fell into step at his side, casting me worried glances. Willets' blood was splattered on her cheek. My stomach dropped as I looked at her. She wasn't supposed to be here to see all of this. I had failed in keeping her safe.

By the time we reached the end of the tunnel I was leaning heavily on Triven for support. Sweat was beading on my forehead. Despite my anger for inadvertently bringing Mouse along, it was a good thing we had her. Just like at the entrance, there was also a keypad hidden here. As Mouse's fingers reached for the keys, the pressure in the tunnel suddenly shifted, my ears popping with the change.

"Extinguish the lights," I hissed. Triven switched his off immediately. After only a moment of hesitation, Brant or Grant or whatever his name was followed suit. No sooner had his torch gone out than the voices reached our ears.

The Ravagers were in the tunnel.

I could hear Mouse's finger tapping feverishly on the keypad. There was another mechanical beep followed by a series of clicks and the door popped open letting in another rush of air. If we had felt their entrance, they would surely feel our escape. The footfalls coming from the end of the tunnel were moving faster now, the voices growing louder.

"Run," I said through gritted teeth. Fighting off the pain and the fatigue I pushed forward. Fumbling in the darkness I found Mouse's frail shoulders as other hands pushed us forward into the unknown.

I half expected to find a firing squad waiting for us on the other side, but as we stumbled into the open cavernous room, it was clear we were alone. Mouse struggled free from my grip. Grabbing my good hand she began to pull me through the foreign space. The room was filled with pipes, ranging in size from an inch to nearly ten feet in diameter. There was a constant buzzing that made my skin crawl. I realized vaguely that it was electricity. We were inside the powerhouse to The Wall.

We had made it barely twenty feet before a deafening automated screeching filled the air. They knew we were here. I wanted to stop and cover my ears but Mouse kept moving. I glanced back to see Triven, Maddox and what's his name running behind us. Each had his gun drawn, but their faces were screwed up against the painful noise.

Triven shouted something at me but I couldn't hear him over the noise.

Mouse stopped outside of a huge vat and pointed animatedly to the round valve on the hatch. Maddox reached us first, pushing me aside to turn the valve. It finally gave way as Triven joined him. The huge metal door swung open and without hesitation Mouse dashed inside. I moved quickly after her, sharing a look of concern with Triven as I passed him.

Where was she taking us?

The vat door slammed closed, its heavy thud drowned out by the blaring alarms. At first I thought we were trapped, but then I caught sight of movement above us. Mouse was hanging on a ladder dangling just above my head. She motioned for me to follow. I couldn't see the top and there was no way of knowing just how high we would have to climb. I grimaced as my shoulder throbbed. Any other time and I could have scaled the ladder no problem. But my hands were slick with blood and I could feel more of it still seeping out of the gunshot wound on my arm. The blonde guard pushed passed me and began to climb. Maddox threw me a resentful look, before following his friend.

"Can you make it?" Triven whispered in my ear.

I gritted my teeth. "Is there any other choice?"

Before he could offer to carry me— which surely meant we would both fall— I wiped my hands on my thighs and began to climb. My shoulder seared with every movement. I was less than ten feet up when my vision began to swim with tears of pain. Despite my anger and determination they continued to fall. I could feel Triven's hands near my feet, moving each time I moved.

I should have made him go first. I was slowing him down and now if I fell I would likely knock him off.

As we rose, the screaming sirens fell away, leaving only the ringing in my ears. My hands had begun to fail, the numbness in my right hand making it impossible to hold onto the rails. I began wrapping my arm through the bars, using the crook of my elbow to hold me steady. I could see a light now. It was not so much a light, I supposed, but more of less dense blackness. In my haste to reach it my foot slipped. A startled cry escaped as my arm lost its hold. Stars burst into my vision as my chin struck one of the rails, smacking my teeth violently together. By of some miracle my left hand kept its grasp as I dangled in the air. Hands shoved my feet back on a rail and suddenly a warm chest was pressed tightly against the back of my legs holding them in place.

"Thank you." I said breathlessly.

"We're almost there." He whispered, equally winded. "You have to keep moving."

He didn't call me weak or offer to carry me. Instead he knew what I needed— words that would push me.

With the little strength I had left, I made my arm link around the metal rail again and pulled. The progression was slow and painful, but somehow I managed to move upwards.

Whenever my foot slipped Triven's hand caught it, pushing me upwards again. We were almost there. I could see it, an opening in the metal ceiling.

My vision was beginning to blur, blackness creeping its way into the edges. Suddenly, the opening that had seemed so close was slipping further away. I could hear Triven's voice behind me but his words didn't register. Overly large, thick hands appeared in the opening. I tried to recoil as they reached for me, but as I moved the world around me began to slip away. The rails disappeared beneath my hands and I was falling.

***

The ringing in my ears told me I was still alive, but my eyes struggled to open. The ground beneath me was shaking, the strange vibrations causing my arm to ache. I could hear voices talking quietly, someone saying my name.

"I think she's waking up."

"Great." Someone muttered not sounding altogether enthused.

"Phoenix, can you hear me?"

I moaned in response. "What the *hell* happened?"

My jaw hurt.

There was a low laugh. "That a girl."

Lips brushed my forehead. The ground beneath me stopped shaking, but as my senses returned I realized my head wasn't resting on the ground. It was being cradled in a small lap. Two little hands were running methodically through my hair, trying to soothe me. When I finally got my eyes to open, Mouse was staring down at me. Tears stained her flushed cheeks. I reached up with my good hand to wipe them away.

"Hey, it's alright. I'm just fine." She nodded, more tears welling in her eyes.

With Triven's help I sat up, wincing as my arm moved.

"Where are we?" I glanced around at the tunnel we were crouched in. There was a walkway about the size of a city

185

sidewalk and maybe fifteen pipes of various colors that ran along next to it. There were dim oval-shaped lights that flanked the wall. Unlike our green-hued ones, these set off a warm amber color. Maddox and the blonde sat twenty feet down from us, speaking in hushed tones.

"We're under the city." As if on cue, something rumbled past on the streets above us. We all jumped looking towards the curved ceilings. "We are going to have to hole up here for a little while. The sun will be coming up soon and the streets will be teeming with soldiers."

Triven ran his hand through his hair. I understood what he wasn't saying aloud. We were trapped in a city with no way out and we were being hunted. The only people who knew how to help us were most likely dead and our lives were being held in the hands of a scared little girl. In other words the reaper was already stalking us in the shadows, he was just waiting for our hearts to officially stop beating.

"Did you stop the bleeding?" I glanced down at my arm, trying not to think about our impending deaths.

"I was able to staunch it, but I'm afraid if your heart rate rises again the patch won't hold."

"Doc put a kit in my bag, there's got to be something in there." Mouse jumped up, scampering to find my bag. I touched my chin, my hand coming back slick. "How far did I fall down the shaft?"

I vaguely remembered those few moments before I had blacked out.

"Maddox and I caught you before you fell, but you managed to hit your chin pretty hard before that. You split it pretty badly."

As my vision continued to clear, I looked harder at Triven. There was blood smeared on his cheek and his hands were tinged red. I was sure there was blood coating his clothing as well, but the black fabric hid any trace of it. He looked tired, his bright eyes dimmer than usual. Mouse returned with my bag and I reluctantly looked away from his face. After rifling through its contents, Triven came up with a small silver tin. Inside Doc had packed three bottles of green serum, a suture kit, a roll of bandages and several small blue pills. While I had no clue what the majority of those things were, relief washed over Triven's face as he looked over the supplies.

He smiled. "That Doc is a good man."

He pulled out one of the green vials and began stripping away the bandages on my arm. Mouse grabbed my other hand in support. The wound looked worse than I had imagined. The bullet had gone straight through, but the skin around the opening had turned a sickly grey color. Though I knew little about medicine, I knew it wasn't good.

"This is going to burn, but then it should get better. Normally I would sedate you, but we don't have anything." Triven's hand shook a little as he held the vial over my arm. His other hand clasped down on my collarbone to hold me steady. I could see the regret in his hazel eyes.

Never taking my eyes from his, I nodded, gritting my teeth. "Do it."

Burn was an understatement. My entire body seized as the green ooze came in contact with my open flesh. It felt like he had just shoved a hot poker into my arm. Pain radiated out from the wound, pulsing though my body with a heartbeat of its own. It took everything I had not to scream. Mouse's hand closed tighter around mine and I closed my eyes as they rolled back into my head. I didn't want to scare her further. The pain seared until I could feel nothing else but the flames. Eventually, I could feel Triven's hand on my chest and the pain began to recede.

When I opened my eyes again there were fresh tears on my cheeks, but my head had seemed to clear. I glanced at my arm in shock. Where there had been torn flesh and exposed muscle tissue, there was now only a perfectly round scab about the size of my thumb. Tentatively, I ran my hand over the raised flesh. It was hot to the touch, but the pain was a fraction of what it was. What was once unbearable now felt like an old, achy wound. I turned my stunned gaze to Triven's.

"Amazing, isn't it? One of Doc's own inventions. Burns like hell, but kills off all infection in the process. Its healing qualities are not quite as good as the regeneration serum, but it's still better than sutures."

"We should get moving." I tried to push myself up but Triven held me down.

"It's been a long night and we have an even longer one ahead of us. Mouse says we're safe here for now and I think it's best if we all eat and rehydrate. Besides, I think we need a new plan."

"They knew we were coming." I whispered to him, shooting a sideways glance in Maddox and Brant's— I might as well call him something— direction.

Triven followed my gaze.

"I know." He whispered before finding us something to eat.

22. SET

The MREs tasted horrible after eating home-cooked meals over the past weeks. A few months ago and this meal would have been a delicacy, but now it was hard to stomach. Mouse never left my side as we ate, her worried eyes darting continually to mine. Doc's serum worked magic on my body. What had once felt feverous and weak, now felt rejuvenated. Even the cut on my chin had scabbed over with surprising speed. It seemed like such a waste of talent, that a man like Doc Porters was residing in an underground culture with limited resources. If he had access to the machines and technology here, his potential would be endless. I wondered vaguely what would make a man of his talents leave a place like this, if his reason had been like my parents' or if they were his own. Either way, I would never know. My parents' reasons died with them and we would be lucky to see tomorrow, much less Doc again.

By the time I finished my meal— an old habit of never wasting anything, no matter how bad it tasted— I noticed Mouse had barely touched hers. More food had been pushed around than actually eaten. Upon meeting my gaze her eyes filled with tears again. She set aside her food and signed. *I'm sorry.* The pain was clear on her round face. Glancing up, I saw that Triven and the other two men were bent in conversation as they heated their meals.

I spoke in a low voice as to not call attention to us. "You knew this would happen didn't you? That we would be ambushed?"

She shook her head. I could tell she was being truthful.

"But you thought this might happen?"

She nodded, her bottom lip trembling.

"You wanted to protect us." I knew this even without her answer. Mouse wasn't trying to be defiant before; she was trying to help us.

"Is there another way out of here?" The men's murmurs had stopped. They were listening now.

She nodded again, but I could see the hesitation behind her eyes. There may be another way out, but our chances weren't good and it wasn't going to be easy. It also didn't escape my attention that she was scared, though I couldn't be sure if it was because of the situation we were now in or because she was back inside The Sanctuary.

"We can't get there from here, can we?"

She shook her head.

"We have to go up to the surface." I assumed and she nodded, confirming my thoughts. I opened my mouth to ask her another question, but it never made it past my lips.

Brant what's-his-face jumped to his feet, descending on us with alarming intensity. Triven was only steps behind him, both of their meals forgotten on the ground. Maddox picked up Triven's and began to eat it, obviously unconcerned.

"Why the hell are we listening to this little misfit? She's the one that got us into this freaking mess in the first place. Don't touch me!" He shook off Triven's warning hand. "All we have done is listen to this brat and look where we are! Stuck in a freaking drainage system while being hunted by enemies we know almost nothing about, not to mention the fact that the rest of our team now lies dead in the Ravagers' back alley. I say screw the kid. She got us in this. Hell she might even be the cause of it, so she should get us out. She's the one they want anyway! If we just hand her over, maybe they will give us asylum—"

I had had enough. His fat little sausage finger was pointed at Mouse's terrified face. Even in my depleted state I was faster than he was. In one bound, I threw Mouse protectively behind me and grabbed his finger, bending it so far backwards I could feel the bones threatening to break. The massive blonde guard fell to his knees before me, twisting to try and free himself. But I held fast.

My voice was perfectly even when I spoke. "We will be moving forward with the plan as instructed by Arstid with one amendment. We will acquire civilian uniforms and blend in. While topside we will gather as much information as we can, but our main objective now is to escape. Together. We are sitting ducks here and this little girl is our only hope of getting out. If you come anywhere near her, if you so much as look at her wrong, or even look like you're thinking about betraying us, I will put a bullet in your head. No hesitation. Got it?"

I bent his finger back further emphasizing my point.

He screamed through his teeth. "Got it! I GOT IT!"

I set him free and began packing my bag. "We leave on the hour."

***

Triven had said nothing about my outburst and Maddox seemed to find it more amusing than threatening. Still, Brant had shut his mouth and fell in line like a good little soldier. But one of us always had an eye on him just in case.

Moving had given me a sense of accomplishment but now standing in wait as a ten-year-old child stole clothing for us made my whole body ache with anxiety. We were stopped at the dead end of a large tunnel. A ladder with a blue wave symbol painted on its side was the only way of escape. I had had to watch Mouse disappear up the ladder with nothing more on her than the knife I had hidden in her boot. I had tried to insist on coming with her but she had relentlessly refused me, signing over and over again, *danger*. I had left her with a final warning that if she wasn't back within fifteen minutes I was coming after her guns blazing. To make my attitude worse, as Mouse disappeared, Brant had muttered something about "That's the last we'll ever see of her."

I seriously thought about breaking his nose.

At eight minutes and forty-three seconds Mouse's feet reappeared on the ladder rungs. She was grinning, clearly proud of herself. She had managed to procure a linen bag nearly as big as herself and in it were differing colors of uniforms for each of us.

Triven gathered her into his arms, kissing the top of her head. "Good job kiddo. You might have just saved us all."

Brant rolled his eyes, but when he caught the expression on my face he quickly grabbed his blue workman uniform and retreated further down the tunnel to change. The clothing was all loosely sewn, allowing us to keep our fatigues on under them. Triven, Mouse and I were all dressed alike in white linen civilian uniforms. The flowy garbs were identical with no distinction between the male and female, except for the cut in the tunic. Triven's tunic was broader in the shoulders whereas mine was cut wide below the waist allowing for the hips I didn't have. The pants were a simple plain white linen that came down to our toes with a drawstring waist. I had to roll the tops of mine twice to accommodate my shorter legs. The tunics were equally loose, falling just past our knees, giving away little of a person's shape, which in our case was great for concealing weapons. In our favor there were also deep hoods that once pulled up concealed our faces nicely. Maddox and Brant, however, were less lucky.

The workmen's uniforms were more like jumpsuits. Like ours they were loose-fitting, but they were one solid piece with a single zipper up the front. Good for concealing weapons, bad for retrieving them. They were also sans hoods, leaving their faces exposed. Brant's uniform was a dark blue, which Arstid had informed us, was water maintenance. Maddox wore one of dark green, indicating a yard and garden worker. Mouse pointed to Brant's long hair and mimed tucking it into his collar. Mumbling something unintelligible he followed the instructions. Triven tossed the now empty bag at Brant.

"You can hide your packs in this. Plus it wouldn't hurt to put in a few weapons that you might need as a last resort." He turned back to us and laid the map in front of Mouse. "How far do we need to go?"

She squinted at the map and pointed to a large building on the far northwest corner. The building was significantly larger than the others around it. I remembered Arstid marking it as a government building of sorts.

"Where are we now?" I traced the city lines, mapping out all direct accesses.

Mouse poured over the map, but looked confused. We had worried that the city might have changed over the years and from the look on Mouse's face it had. Eventually, she shrugged and circled a general vicinity with her finger. Rocking back on my heels I let out a shallow breath. If she was right, we were a few hours walk from the destination. We would be cutting it close with the curfew. If we could run it, the timing wouldn't be an issue, but we had to blend in, so sprinting through the city was not an option. I glanced up to find Triven's eyes on me. I could see the same thoughts running through his mind as well. After I had committed our general route to memory, Triven folded the map and slipped it into his breast pocket.

We ascended the ladder in silence, Mouse leading the way. At the top was a metal door that she easily pushed aside and scrambled out. As I emerged from the hole, I understood why Mouse had picked this specific hatch over the others we had passed and how she had acquired the uniforms so quickly. The access panel we had just crawled out of ended in some kind of laundry depository. The air smelled faintly of bleach and cleaning chemicals and was sticky with moisture. Piled in neat little groupings in front of their coordinating colored bay doors, were stacks of clean uniforms. There were a few windows, but they were all high up on the walls and clouded over with years of dust and steam. A dim glow was the only thing visible through them. Voices could be heard coming from the front of the building. Mouse pointed towards the blue set of bay doors and we moved out.

Triven glided through the warehouse silently. Watching him move was mesmerizing. The few times we had run rooftops together, he had let me take lead. But now, following behind him, I was amazed by his sense of body. He moved with a grace I wasn't sure I could ever possess. I shook the thought from my mind as he reached the metal door. To our shock there weren't locks on any of the doors, it was as if security wasn't an issue here, although clothing here obviously wasn't the commodity it was in Tartarus. Lifting in unison, Triven and I pushed the door up just high enough for us to slip under. A bright light poured in from the outside. Every muscle in my body tensed as I waited for an alarm to rise or the metal door to squeak in protest, but nothing happened.

Triven pointed to us in turn. "Maddox, you will take lead. After a thirty-second count Bowen will follow—" *Guess his name wasn't Brant after all.* "The three of us will be behind you in another thirty. Take your cues from the people around you. It is imperative that we blend in. Eyes open and stay sharp. If you can get a count on soldiers and weapons even better."

He paused.

"If something happens, if someone approaches you, stay calm. The main goal is to get out alive. If we get separated keep moving north by northwest."

With a nod Maddox dropped and rolled through the gap disappearing from sight. We held for thirty count, which I spent glaring a warning at Brant— I was just going to call him that anyway. When he disappeared Triven took my hand squeezing it tightly.

194

I squeezed back.

On thirty I moved first. Dropping low, I rolled over the threshold and slumped silently to the ground. The instant my feet hit, I recoiled covering my eyes. I could hear the noises of the street nearby, but the blinding light was so painful I knew we must be under attack. Hastily, I pulled the gun from my belt and aimed into the unseen. What the hell had we just walked into?

I barely heard the feet hit the ground next to me, but I recognized Triven's hands as they wrapped over mine. They forced my hands down concealing the gun as he whispered in my ear.

"It's okay, Prea. It's just the sun, give your eyes a moment to adjust."

The sun? But it was too bright. Even as the thought crossed my mind, the alley we stood in came into better view. I could see outlines, then the building's bricks, then Triven's face next to mine. Mouse was protectively hidden behind his back. My finger came off the trigger instantly. The tension left both their bodies as mine relaxed.

The sun.

I glanced up at the sky shielding my eyes with my hand. The glowing orb was set in a crystal blue sky. I had a flash of memory like this. Not anything of importance, just my fingers outlined in the bright light. After living the last six years practically in darkness, the sun seemed foreign. The few rare glimpses I had caught in Tartarus, the sun was always tainted with sickly pollution, always a muted green. But this bright yellow burst of light was magnificent. My skin even felt the warmth coming from it. How strange.

"Sorry." I muttered in embarrassment. I should have known that it was the sun. I should have expected it. Holstering my weapon, I straightened from my crouch and turned toward the mouth of the alley. As bright as I had first perceived it to be, we were actually in the shadow of the buildings. On the street, people in uniforms similar to ours were moving by slowly. Occasionally a strange vehicle would whirr past, stirring up the air around us. No one even glanced our way. In the distance I could just make out Brant's blue-cladded back.

Pulling our hoods up, the three of us moved towards the mouth of the alley. As we neared the opening Mouse slipped her hands into ours. If anyone were to glance at us, we would look like a happy family out for a stroll. Stepping out just as a group of civilians passed, we merged into the crowds unnoticed. My instincts told me to keep my eyes down, not to make eye contact, but remembering what Triven said about taking *their* lead made me think better of it. Strangely, as every person passed one another they would glance briefly into each other's eyes and incline their heads politely. In less than thirty yards I had nodded at about twenty people. If the streets were teaming, this social custom would be ludicrous. When we finally came to a stretch with fewer pedestrians I got a better look at the city.

The buildings were all painted varying tones of beige and white. Everything was a soft muted tone that should have pleased the eyes, but to me they only seemed to reflect the blinding sun more. I focused hard on not blinking too much, but my eyes had begun to water slightly. Up ahead I could see Maddox turn a corner. Then Brant. At our set pace, we would be less than a minute behind them.

The people here looked equally as simple as the buildings. Those who had their heads exposed wore modest hair. There were absolutely no visible tattoos or piercings to be seen. In fact, there was very little to tell them apart from one another. I was so used to seeing the defining features of the Tribes, that here it seemed as if everyone had no identity at all. Every passing face just blurred into the next one. The only thing defining a person was the color of the uniform they wore. To my dismay, we passed every colored uniform except one. In the array of muted tones, we never passed a single silver one. Silver was the color of their guard, of their trained army men. I had expected the streets to be teaming with guards, seeing as how our arrival had not been so quiet. But there was not a single armed guard in sight. Their lack of presence alarmed me just as much as it comforted me. If they weren't here, then where were they?

We turned another corner and both Maddox and Brant came back into view. As much as I disliked both of them, I felt a sense of ease seeing familiar figures again.

It was painful moving so slowly, almost as if each second ticking by brought the knife hanging over our heads closer. Mouse's hand grew clammy in mine, but neither of us were bold enough to let go and wipe away the sweat. Our progression became like a choreographed dance.

Step, step, nod. Step, step, scan. Step, step, nod. Step, step, scan.

These regulated movements repeated themselves over and over again, until I was barely aware I was doing it. We had gone twenty-three blocks and the sun was starting to ride low on the horizon. At this rate we were not going to make it before the citywide curfew, but if we moved any faster we would stand out in the dwindling crowd. And if we weren't undercover by curfew, then we were sure as dead. Plans started formulating in my head, but they were quickly interrupted. As we turned the next corner, my knees locked.

Ahead I could see Maddox's green suit slowing as he neared the mouth of an alley. Twenty yards behind him, Brant stood frozen as two men in silver uniforms hailed him. We couldn't hear their conversation, but as they grew closer Brant moved his hand to his pocket. Unbeknownst to the guards, the bottom of the pocket had been cut and his hand was resting on the gun attached to his thigh. The guards' weapons were still slung casually over their shoulders. Clearly whatever they wanted, they did not perceive him as a threat. But it was clear even from a distance the feeling was not mutual. Brant's hand twitched. My free hand moved to my gun as well.

"Be calm." I heard Triven mutter under his breath.

I couldn't tell if he was talking to me or warning Brant.

Mouse's hand tightened in mine as the guards drew even with him. Several words were exchanged and the three of us stopped breathing. Even Maddox had stopped with his back still to us. Then without a warning the two guards nodded and began to walk away. My body went slack as relief filled the air, Mouse's tiny hand loosening. We were okay. They were walking away. Less than five feet away, one guard turned to glance back and then Brant's gun went off.

23. MATCH

It took a moment, a heartbeat, to realize what had happened. As the guard's head whipped back and his slack body crumpled to the ground, time seemed to stand still. Then all at once it sped up, as if making up for the lost seconds. The second guard glanced at his dead comrade in shock, but his training quickly took over as he turned his firearm on Brant.

Gunfire echoed down the streets like sporadic thunder. I felt sickly vindicated having not wasted any brain cells remembering his name as Brant's body spasmed when the bullets pierced his flesh. Obviously our outdated armor was nothing compared to their weapons. None of us were safe now.

While he shot, the guard was screaming into his earpiece. He would not be alone for long. In the short instant that his gunfire ceased, his cold blue eyes turned instantly to us. In that instant there was understanding in his eyes and I knew we had made a mistake.

Every other civilian still on the streets had dropped to their knees at the sound of the first shot. Hoods were pushed back from their plain faces and their hands were locked behind their heads. They had been trained to show they were disarmed, to surrender immediately. Only four people still stood on the street and now the guard knew exactly who we were. His gun rose, the barrel pointed at my face, but the shot that rang out didn't come from him. Maddox had fired, hitting the guard's left shoulder. Without hesitation, we bolted for the nearest alley. As we dove into the shadows, I caught Maddox's green jump suit disappearing into another alleyway.

My instinct was to go higher, but the roofs here were sloped too steeply to maneuver. My eyes searched the ground, but the even pavement had no drains. There was nowhere to hide and the darkness was creeping in at an unusually rapid rate. The white linens we had donned to hide would soon make us easy targets. We shed our stolen clothing as we sprinted through alley. I pulled at Mouse, helping her out of disguise before removing my own. Once free of his garb, Triven grabbed Mouse, swinging her up into his arms as he ran. Our eyes met for a second and a horrible flash passed through my mind. I had lived this moment before, but through different eyes. The only difference was that I was no longer the one being carried. This time I was in my parents' shoes.

I pushed harder, running from my past. Running for their lives as well as our own.

The darkness had swallowed the city whole, almost as if by command. The thought flickered through my mind that maybe that's exactly what had happened. If they could make the sun so bright here, the usually tarnished skies so blue, then wasn't it just as possible that they could take that all away? The shields surrounding the city kept us out, but they were also keeping these people in, controlling their lives.

Even in our fear-driven panic, we ran with purpose. Every turn we took kept us on a path toward the northwest corner of the city. We just had to keep moving. The alleys here were cleaner than ours. The pavement was smooth and uncluttered with trash and rubble. The catch was if we could move faster, so could the people chasing us.

I turned a corner three steps ahead of Triven and collided with a wall of human flesh. The world spun as I was knocked to ground, but not before I could pull the knife from my boot. I slashed out as our bodies collided with the cement, but found only air. I thrust again, but a meaty hand closed over my wrist, squeezing so hard I could feel the bones bend, precariously close to snapping.

"Now is that any way to greet a friend?"

I kicked, catching Maddox in the gut and throwing him off of me. I grabbed my newly healed arm as it began throbbing again. It felt as if the wound may have reopened. "No, that's how I greet everyone I hate."

Triven pulled back his gun as he recognized our lost teammate. "No time for reunions. We have to move."

He was right. There were new sounds in the air now. Pounding footsteps could now be heard in the distance. They were accompanied by the strange humming I had heard from the passing vehicles we saw earlier. They were closing in. We launched into motion only to come to a dead stop at the mouth of the next alley.

The once tightly knit city buildings fell away from one another. The alleys we sought for cover were no longer feet away but blocks. A strange plot of green grass and trees had been dropped in the middle of the city and the only way to escape was through the exposed land. The feet were getting closer.

"Move!" I yelled bursting into the open.

The area was oddly maintained and had an intentionally paved path winding its way though the manicured grass. I ignored it and cut straight across the slippery, spongy surface seeking the most direct path I could find.

Thirty feet.

A gun shot.

Twenty-five feet.

A returned gun shot.

Fifteen feet.

I came to a dead halt. Standing in the middle of the alley I was aiming for was a guard, gun raised ready to fire. His finger twitched on the trigger, but I was faster. As I fired, two more shots rang out. I spun just in time to see two other guards fall as Maddox and Triven lowered their guns. As I turned, another two guards appeared in a different alley. Maddox and I fired.

Panic rose in my chest. They had chased us into a trap. We were standing in the center of a hexagon and every way out had soldiers charging towards us. I could hear them. Triven set Mouse down and tried to shield her as his gun jumped from alley to alley. The knife I gave her was clutched in her tiny shaking hand. Even Maddox's shoulders fell as he comprehended the severity of the situation.

It was over.

I staggered backwards as the realization hit me and faltered. My feet hit something uneven and a glimmer of hope ran through me. I clawed at the ground feeling my nails break as they scraped the metal surface. Joy pulsed through me. It was a grate. There was a chance of escape.

"Help me!" I screamed.

Triven's hands were instantly next to mine pulling at the metal grate. Maddox fired twice more.

"Hurry it up sweetheart they're coming faster." He growled over his shoulder.

With a heave the grate came free, swinging upward. There was no ladder, we would have to jump. I quickly dropped my backpack in to test the depth. It hit ground after only a short fall; it couldn't be more than ten feet. There were three more shots. Triven held the grate back, staring at me.

"GO!" He screamed.

I shook my head, "I can't catch Mouse, I can barely use my arm. You have to go first."

Pain flashed in eyes.

Two more shots.

"I'll be right behind you." I touched his face. He cupped his hand over mine and disappeared into the hole. I could hear his feet hit.

"Drop her to me!"

Three more shots.

I grabbed Mouse and kissed her forehead. Taking her by the wrists I lowered her as far as I could before letting go.

"Okay your turn!" Triven shouted up to me, I could just make out his face in the darkness. I raised my head. A sea of silver was descending down the alleys now. Maddox's gun was firing wildly into the onslaught, but more soldiers just replaced the fallen ones. I heard the click as his clip emptied. I glanced down at my chest. A tiny red light had appeared over my heart. There wasn't time to save all of us but I could save two of us. They just needed a head start and I could provide them with that. I couldn't give them much, but I could give them time.

"I'm sorry." The words were barely a whisper but Triven heard them.

"Prea!" He screamed and I shut the grate.

I rose to face the gun that was pointed straight at my heart as the resounding bang rang out. The guard's aim was true and he would not miss. I knew I wouldn't even have time to brace myself and it didn't matter as long as it saved them. Something large blocked my line of sight and I was flung to the ground. My head smacked against the ground with surprising force. No sooner did I hit the pavement than something pierced the flesh in my lower back. My body began to seize, my limbs flailing uncontrollably as electricity rushed through them. Everything burned even when the convulsions stopped, my limbs refusing to move. Something fell next to me, the sound sickening as hard surface met skull bone. With great effort, I turned my head toward the body next to mine.

Maddox lay facedown on the pavement, his black eyes wild as they turned to me. He opened his mouth to speak, but instead of words a river of blood poured over his white lips. Realization crashed down like lead rain.

He had taken the bullet meant for me.

His hand crept toward me, his fingers reaching out.

Blood was pooling beneath him, seeping out and staining the pristine pavement. Something I had never seen passed across his hardened face. Fear.

Ignoring the pain still radiating through my body, I reached out and grabbed his hand. His massive hand shook beneath mine. His mouth opened and closed like a fish out of water. The calloused fingers wrapped around mine squeezing so tightly it hurt. I squeezed back, letting him know I was here, that he wasn't alone. I squeezed until his grip loosened and the life left his black eyes. The man I hated with all my being, had just given his life for mine. I squeezed even after he let go, after there was nothing left but a body. Even when I finally had to turn my eyes away, I didn't let go of his hand.

The street flooded with spotlights, filling the once blackened night with light. I blinked. A thousand red dots swam around me as the guards put me in their sights. Raising my hands above my head, I held my open palms to oncoming soldiers and for the first time in my life I surrendered. Not to save myself, but to buy Triven and Mouse time.

I pressed my face into the grate beneath me. A perfect face stared back at me from the shadows, horror and pain evident in his eyes. I could see him clearly now in the artificial lights cast down on us. I could even see the cherubic face of the tiny girl clinging to his side.

He began to try and climb up, to push against the grate, but I shook my head. It took all of my effort to speak and not cry.

"Save her."

At first I didn't think he heard my words, but after a few excruciatingly long seconds he nodded. Tears marred his perfect eyes before they steeled.

"Survive Prea. I *will* come back for you. Don't you dare die on me." And then he was gone.

A different kind of pain tore through me as the rough hands found me. I realized as they pulled me away from the grate, that they were taking me away from the only two people

I ever loved. I steeled myself with that realization.

For them I would find the strength, I would rise above my own fears.

I would survive this new world, and I *would* find a way back to them.

ACKNOWLEDGEMENTS:

Writing a book involves so many more people than just the author. While I supplied the passion for *New World: Rising,* so many others helped bring my dream to fruition. I realize that some will never read these pages— heaven knows I have skipped my fair share of acknowledgments— but for those who do, I want them to know how thankful I am for everyone who contributed to my first novel.

First and foremost, thanks to *you*, my readers. Without your interest, my book would just be sitting on a hard drive collecting digital dust. No matter how much I advertise or beg bookstores to sell my book, it is your word of mouth that drives others to read Phoenix's story. And for that I am eternally grateful. I gave Phoenix life but you have kept her alive. I ask one more favor of you, my readers. While passion consumes me to write, I am still human and thus make mistakes. If you find errors in my book, please contact me so I can correct them.

To my confidants, editors and beta-readers: Diane Schultz, Auston Wilson, Cameron Walker, Kimberly Karli, Cerri Norris, Annette Meyerkord and Rachel Walkskey. Without your keen eyes, challenging questions and encouragement I never could have developed this story into what it is today. It is an honor to have all of you in my life and to have been able to share the inner workings of my mind with you. Thank you for your invaluable advice, kind words and honesty. I could not have done this without you.

To my incredible multimedia team over at Studio Hippo, thank you for your hard work and creative souls that brought my story to life on the web. You took my words and produced an amazing book trailer that makes my skin tingle with excitement every time I watch it.

To my husband for his never-ending patience and encouragement. You are my best friend, my muse, my rock.

The best day of my life was the day you walked into it. With you by my side, my dreams have become a reality and I want nothing more than to share them with you. You have spent many nights letting me be antisocial so I could write, listened to me cry over rejection letters, reminded me to sleep when I needed to stop obsessing and rest, and finally got me to stop saying "I can't." You never cease to amaze and inspire me. I love you.

Lastly, but certainly never least, thank you to my family. Sara, you have not only been my sister but a best friend. You helped bring so many great books into my life that have inspired me. Without your encouragement to read, I could never have found the inspiration to write my own book. Mom and Dad, you raised me to be a strong, confident woman. You taught me to be patient, to be kind, to respect others, and most of all to believe in myself. Everything I am today is because of you. While most people fear becoming their parents when they get older, I would consider it an honor.

Stay tuned for the second book in the *New World*
series:

New World: Ashes
Coming soon…

40427688R00137

Made in the USA
Lexington, KY
05 April 2015